Quick As A Flash, Vivian Hit The Switch, And The Room Went Mercifully Black.

"You must be the sister-in-law," he murmured dryly. "The one who didn't want to meet me."

"No! I'm not her! And I don't know her. And you don't, either," she replied, panicked.

Vivian moved away from the wall and began to fumble frantically in the dark for her bathrobe, cursing when her fingers were shaking too violently to pull it on.

Bedsheets rustled. Not good.

"You stay right where you are!" she screeched, backing toward the shower.

"I like the light better on," he said. "The view was better."

"Well, I don't. And I don't want to know who you are."

"The name's Cash McRay. And I damn sure want to know the name of the naked lady who saved me from my nightmare. I was drenched in sweat from terror—and there you were, like Venus arising from the sea—to rescue me. Exquisite Aphrodite."

She groaned aloud. Now her future brother-in-law had seen her in her birthday suit!

Dear Reader,

Welcome to another passion-filled month at Silhouette Desire—where we guarantee powerful and provocative love stories you are sure to enjoy. We continue our fabulous DYNASTIES: THE DANFORTHS series with Kristi Gold's *Challenged by the Sheikh*—her intensely ardent hero will put your senses on overload. More hot heroes are on the horizon when *USA TODAY* bestselling author Ann Major returns to Silhouette Desire with the dramatic story of *The Bride Tamer*.

Ever wonder what it would be like to be a man's mistress—even just for pretend? Well, the heroine of Katherine Garbera's *Mistress Minded* finds herself just in that predicament when she agrees to help out her sexy-as-sin boss in the next KING OF HEARTS title. Jennifer Greene brings us the second story in THE SCENT OF LAVENDER, her compelling series about the Campbell sisters, with *Wild In the Moonlight*—and this is one hero to go wild for! If it's a heartbreaker you're looking for, look no farther than *Hold Me Tight* by Cait London as she continues her HEARTBREAKERS miniseries with this tale of one sexy male specimen on the loose. And looking for a little *Hot Contact* himself is the hero of Susan Crosby's latest book in her BEHIND CLOSED DOORS series; this sinfully seductive police investigator always gets his woman! Thank goodness.

And thank *you* for coming back to Silhouette Desire every month. Be sure to join us next month for *New York Times* bestselling author Lisa Jackson's *Best-Kept Lies,* the highly anticipated conclusion to her wildly popular series THE McCAFFERTYS.

Keep on reading!

Melissa Jeglinski

Melissa Jeglinski
Senior Editor, Silhouette Desire

Please address questions and book requests to:
Silhouette Reader Service
U.S.: 3010 Walden Ave., P.O. Box 1325, Buffalo, NY 14269
Canadian: P.O. Box 609, Fort Erie, Ont. L2A 5X3

ANN MAJOR

THE BRIDE TAMER

Silhouette®

Desire

Published by Silhouette Books

America's Publisher of Contemporary Romance

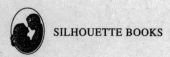 SILHOUETTE BOOKS

ISBN 0-373-76586-X

THE BRIDE TAMER

Books by Ann Major

ANN MAJOR

lives in Texas with her husband of many years and is the mother of three grown children. She has a master's degree from Texas A&M at Kingsville, Texas, and is a former English teacher. She is a founding board member of the RWA and a frequent speaker at writers' groups.

Ann loves to write; she considers her ability to do so a gift. Her hobbies include hiking in the mountains, sailing, ocean kayaking, traveling and playing the piano. But most of all she enjoys her family.

One
_____

Florence, Italy

"**C**ut them off! Then he'll suffer!"

Cash's hand froze on the auditorium door that led to the parking lot and helipad outside when he heard the screams to emasculate him.

Roger, his personal assistant, peered at the swelling crowd from a nearby window and said far too cheerily, "More and more people are streaming into the plaza. Lucky for you, these are modern times and they aren't wearing swords in scabbards. So, I think it's safe enough for you to run for it—"

"What's the matter with them? They've had months to get used to my design," Cash said.

Cash McRay wasn't a coward. But the roar of five thousand angry Florentines on the other side of the door threatening to cut off precious parts of his body made his blood run cold. His tall angular body felt like an immovable weight as he hesitated. His large, size-twelve feet rooted themselves to the floor.

The death threats grew louder. Hell, maybe he should have played it safe. He'd known the design of the ultra-modern museum was over the top, but had he held back? Hell, no.

"How ironic that the good citizens of Florence want me dead at the precise moment I'd begun to think I might feel like living again someday," he said wryly. Unable to block the memory that had haunted so many of his nightmares, he saw his beloved Susana and little Sophie, lying so still and beyond his reach in their coffins.

Roger placed a hand on Cash's broad back and shoved him forward. "Relax. All the cannibals want is you…on a platter."

Cash whirled, and Roger flashed him the winning smile that had gotten him his job a year ago. Only tonight the kid's snowy white smile made Cash grit his teeth and ball his hands into fists.

"You talk too much," Cash growled. "And you smile too much. It's dangerous. Did anybody ever tell you, you should be a model for a toothpaste ad?"

"Yeah—you! All the time. And it's getting old."

"I'd rather grin goofily for a living than have my testicles served as shish kebab."

"This is good. Finally, a joke from you."

"Life goes on," Cash muttered, determined to believe it.

"Especially since you bumped into Isabela Escobar in Mexico City," Roger said, showing too many teeth again. "Office gossip has it you are going to propose."

"Why do I have to be cursed with the nosiest staff in the world?"

"There have been a lot of perfumed letters."

Cash seethed inwardly. Whether he intended to marry her or not was nobody's business. Aloud he said, "I can't propose to her or anybody else unless you get me out of Florence alive."

Roger threw the door open and pushed him hard. "Run for it, loverboy! I'm right behind you!"

Lowering his head and ducking behind his leather briefcase, Cash dove through the throng that was being held in check behind velvet ropes by beefy security men.

It was early April, and the night air chilled him. The parking lot was jammed. The helipad platform was a hundred yards off to the right. Policemen formed a human barricade all the way to the chain-link fence surrounding it.

When strange hands and arms groped angrily at his legs, he sprinted for the ladder to the helipad, where the black rotors of a jet helicopter chopped a violet sky. Deftly he dodged the microphones that were thrust at his tanned, aristocratic, much-photographed face.

"How could you build such a futuristic monstrosity in a city noted for its architectural beauty and history?" a woman yelled.

"Egotist! Deconstructivist! Modernist! Postmodernist!"

A man with oily black hair rushed him. Fortunately, two guards grabbed the ingrate by the shoulders. "Florence glories in its past," he yelled. "Your museum looks like a crab squatting on a giant toilet!"

Roger smiled and shouted glib answers in his horrendous Italian to the red-faced fellow.

"Did your billionaire daddy bribe the city officials to pick your insane design?" someone else yelled at Cash.

"Avant-garde, please," Roger corrected, his toothy grin as bright as ever.

Stung by the reference to his father, Cash hesitated on the third rung of the ladder and turned just as a rock bounced off his left shoulder.

"No comment!" Roger yelled from a few feet behind him as a hand yanked one of his expensive Italian shoes off. "Climb, Cash, before the natives down here strip me naked! I'm right behind you." More fabric ripped. "Ouch! Let go of my trousers! Hey! The bastard almost got me. Climb! You're not the only one they want to barbecue."

Chain links chimed as a dozen men fought their way over the makeshift fencing. Before the rabble-rousers could reach the ladder, Cash and Roger were in the helicopter. Dozens of flashes went off in their faces. Then the heavy door slammed as the police pulled the climbers off the platform.

Cash leaned back and sighed. Then he jammed his hand in his trouser pocket to make sure the velvet box with Isabela's engagement ring inside was still there.

Isabela was dark and fiery—and so vivaciously alive that maybe she could make him forget his loss. He tried to summon her image. Instead, he saw the still, white features of his wife, Susana, and their precious little daughter, their golden heads gleaming on satin pillows. He heard his stepmother's soft whisper behind him, ordering him to close their caskets.

"You two okay?" Count Leopoldo's soft elegantly accented voice was barely audible over the roar of the helicopter as it took off. "You still game for a private tour of the Galleria degli Uffizi?"

Leopoldo, or rather Leo, and he had roomed together at Harvard.

Cash nodded wearily, his thoughts returning momentarily to the present. The Galleria degli Uffizi was one of the world's great museums of Renaissance art. Susana had never come to Florence without going there....

He turned his head to stare out the window at his creation. In the dying sunlight, from this angle, indeed it did look like a giant golden crab squatting by twin telescopes. As he studied the slanting expanses of gridded glass and the bridges in between the rectangular columns of limestone that had been likened to a crab's legs, he felt a pang of doubt.

The museum was the first thing he'd built since his home in San Francisco had burned. The house he'd designed for Susana had brought much enthusiasm and notoriety and many commissions from all over the world. He'd been away in Europe supervising the renovation of Leo's island retreat when his own house had burned, and he'd lost everything that mattered.

The helicopter shot straight upward into the purple dark, the whir of the rotors drowning out the noise of the crowd. Soon the people in the streets looked like ants. As the helicopter swooped toward the oldest part of the ancient city, all Cash could see were red-tiled roofs, boulevards, squares and the brown glitter of the serpentine Arno, the famous, unpredictable river that had raged through the city on more than one occasion with devastating effect. Florence had survived disasters far worse than one whimsical building.

His old friend Leo had asked if he was okay.

Cash shot Leo a furtive glance. "I forgot what fun it was to be the most hated 'pop' architect on the planet."

"*Controversial* architect," Roger amended. "Hell, this is good. Tomorrow you'll be on the front page of every newspaper in Europe."

"How can you be so damn optimistic—when people want to kill me?"

"My people," Leo began, "Italians, Florentines, we are passionate idiots. You must forgive us. Today we hate you—in four hundred years we will deify you."

Cash glowered. "A lot of good that will do my moldering corpse."

"He wants gloom and doom," Roger said conversationally to Leo. "So, all right, Cash, I'll give you gloom and doom." His pearly smile lit the dark. "You lost the New York proposal."

Cash lowered his head into his hands and experienced the all-too-familiar, bleak, empty sensation of creative despair. He ran his big hands through his shock of thick black hair.

Most people wouldn't have much sympathy for him. Even after Susana's death, everybody had told him he was a fool to mope when he had so much to live for.

"You have your talent, your name, your youth...." *Your money,* they'd meant.

If a man was rich, everybody thought he should be happy. They didn't know. Money, the kind of fortune he possessed, cut him off from almost everybody, from his own humanity even, from feeling anything remotely real. He lived behind walls, sometimes in total isolation. He buried himself in his work.

But his grief was real, and he had regrets like anybody else. He'd loved his wife and child to distraction. If he'd known how little time he had with them, he would never have left them so often to work in all those far-flung places.

People thought because his picture was in magazines, he led a charmed life. "You'll marry again," they said. "A man like you...can have anybody."

At first he'd thought he could never betray Susana by marrying another. But nearly three years had passed, and it was getting harder and harder to live on memories. Two months ago, he'd been in Mexico City visiting his old mentor, Marco Escobar, after he'd had a heart attack. Isabela had popped into her father's hospital room and dropped her shawl. When he'd picked it up, her hand had lingered on his. When she'd shown him sympathy, he'd felt a flicker of interest, the first since his wife's death. And he'd thought maybe...maybe...

"Your Manhattan design was great, Cash. Really," Roger said. "Everybody said so. You're just ahead of your time. Look on the bright side. At least you won't build something that will make Manhattanites scream for your testicles on a skewer, and I won't lose another expensive shoe. New Yorkers are a lot more violent than Italians, you know."

"Maybe. But New Yorkers are a lot more receptive to modern architecture too."

It is always a mistake to retrace one's steps. No sooner was Cash inside the Uffizi than he regretted coming. The walls of the museum that housed the works of the world's finest collection of Italian Renaissance art seemed to close in. The musty odor of the old building and paintings suffocated him.

The memories were still too sharp; Susana's ghost feet too vivid. Only vaguely was he aware of the dimly lit masterpieces, half hidden by glass that loomed above him and Leo in the shadowy gallery.

"The last time I was here, I was with Susana," Cash whispered.

"I know," Leo said, not without sympathy. But he was a man of the world. His first wife had died in a car crash, and he was now on his third marriage—to a beautiful Parisian model.

Leo's heels clicked as he kept walking until they reached a certain gallery in the depths of Galleria degli Uffizi. Suddenly Botticelli's *Birth of Venus* soared above them. Outside the sun had set, and it was raining softly, a spring shower that would soon be over.

The last time he'd been here with Susana, the summer sun had been glorious outside, glorious in her hair, more brilliant and awe-inspiring even than the light in Botticelli's famous paintings. Cash had wanted to stay outside, to walk in the sunny squares with Susana, to feed the pigeons and look at the buildings. But as always, she'd had her heart set on coming here.

He and Susana had honeymooned in Florence. Even on that visit, she'd dragged him out of their bed to visit the Uffizi Palace every afternoon, not because the building was one of the most important examples of Italian Mannerist architecture, but because she'd loved Botticelli so much.

"If Botticelli were alive, I'd be insanely jealous," he'd teased her once.

She'd laughed as she'd run through the galleries ahead of him. And always she'd ended up here, staring at *The Birth of Venus.*

"It's the visual image of the birth of love in the world," she'd explained, sliding her arm through his.

"You're my visual image of love," he'd said.

"It's good you're here again," Leo said, interrupting his reverie. "One must banish ghosts."

"Is that possible?" Cash asked, doubtful.

"I could introduce you to women who are so skilled, they can make a man forget anything...at least for a while."

Cash thought of Isabela and hoped she would be able to do that for him. "You Italians..."

"Men are the same everywhere." Leo paused. "When I saw you at the funeral—"

"Don't."

Again Cash heard his stepmother tell him it was time to close the caskets—and the gallery became as quiet as death for an awkward moment.

"This Venus is one of the most sensuously beautiful nudes painted during the Renaissance," Leo said. "Do you know the myth?"

"The painting is nice."

"Nice? What an awful word—too tame. You Americans overuse it."

"The myth is not so nice. It has some really gruesome aspects."

Leo nodded with a grim little smile, and Cash leaned forward to read a plaque on the wall that told the story. Gaea, mother of Cronus, somehow persuaded the audacious Cronus to castrate his father, Uranus, and throw his severed genitals into the sea.

Cash's gut tightened. Still, he stared up from the little plaque to the breathtaking nude redhead with new interest.

The testicles had floated on the surface of the waters, producing a white foam from which rose the irresistible Aphrodite he saw in the painting. The Romans had adopted the myth, and Botticelli, being Italian, had changed her name to Venus.

According to the plaque, the winds had carried the foam across stormy seas, and she was born along the coast of Cythera. When the foam washed up on the shores of Cyprus, she rose out of the water and presented herself to the gods.

Leo broke the silence. "I always forget how breathtaking Botticelli's Venus is. The gods fell in love with her upon first sight."

Maybe the mood of the painting affected him. For whatever reason, Cash pulled out a little velvet box and snapped it open. "I bought a ring...for Isabela." The diamond flashed at them wickedly.

"Isabela Escobar," Leo purred in his velvet, accented voice.

"She's charming, vivacious and sexy. She makes me laugh."

Leo looked both surprised and impressed. "Smart move, marrying Marco's daughter. More like a merger than a marriage, I'd say."

"It will be a marriage, damn it."

"So—was it love at first sight, this spark between you and fiery Isabela?"

Cash couldn't meet his friend's eyes, and his own voice hardened ever so slightly. "My plane tonight goes to London. And then in a few days I go to the Yucatán peninsula. She lives in Mérida."

"You didn't answer my question."

"As an architect's daughter, she would understand my dreams and my obsession about my work. We share mutual interests and mutual friends. Our love would grow."

"I see," Leo said with way too much understanding.

"Isabela is perfect in every way," Cash persisted a little heatedly. "Love will come—"

"But what if it doesn't? What will you do with your vivacious Isabela then? Leave her behind and amuse yourself with others while you are away working?"

Cash's hand shook as he shut the box and jammed it into his pocket. "I wish I hadn't told you."

"Does *she* know that you intend to ask her?"

"She knows that I'm coming—yes. That I'm going to propose—no."

"You're a fool." Leo laughed. "Women always know these things. Especially a woman like Isabela. She's probably planning the exact spot where you'll propose. There will be moonlight and candlelight and soft music. You'll be at the beach or by a pool and she'll be wearing the sexiest outfit you ever saw. Knowing Isabela, she'll be in black or red, depending on her mood. She'll touch you, and before you know it, she'll have you down on bended knee."

"What does it matter if I'm going to propose, anyway?"

Leo dismissed the matter with a wave of his hand. "If this isn't a merger, and it isn't love at first sight, what propelled you into...this marital adventure?"

"Love at first sight—at my age?" Leo was beginning to annoy him.

"What are you—all of thirty-five?"

"Thirty-eight."

Leo glanced up at the painting again. "I'm afraid the Greeks would beg to differ with you on love at first sight. Troy fell because of this goddess."

"That's just a myth."

"Myths are very powerful. So is love. Life can be very dull if a man doesn't have a grand passion for a beautiful woman."

"Maybe for you Italians. But I am an American."

"The most unromantic people on earth."

"Oh, we have our share of romantic fools. But I'm too old and too practical for that sort of thing."

"How long will your fiery, flirtatious Latina be content with a cold fish for a husband if you don't fall madly in love with her?"

Suddenly the repetitive conversation was bothering the hell out of Cash. But like that cold fish in his friend's metaphor, he was baited by Leo's barbs and couldn't wriggle off the hook. "Life...love...turn out better if you plan them first."

"One should never marry just to marry."

"Maybe no one should ever give anyone else advice," Cash lashed out.

"Too true," Leo conceded in his deep gentle voice. "Congratulations, then."

"I've got a plane to catch to London—"

"Indeed. And then Isabela. And Mexico."

As they began to stroll toward the exit sign, Cash said, "I am going to redesign and rebuild her beach house on the Caribbean. As a wedding gift."

"Wouldn't she rather have…something more personal?" Leo paused as if trying to find a way to phrase his thoughts. "A final warning, my friend. I've spent time in Mexico. It is a land with a powerful mythology and ancient gods."

"What does that have to do with getting married?"

"To go there is to tempt fate."

"What the hell are you trying to say?"

Leo stared at him and shrugged. After that they spoke of inconsequential things. It was pouring when they stepped outside. It had been pouring the day of the funeral too.

In a blinding flash, Cash knew that whether or not he could ever love Isabela, he had to marry.

If he didn't make new memories with someone soon, he'd go mad.

Two

Waves lapped against the hull of Aaron's yacht as Vivian Escobar swirled her crystal flute and tried not to fume. She couldn't believe Aaron, her Spanish student, of all people—sedate, fatherly Aaron—had hit on her and then gone below and expected her to follow.

Did he actually believe she was panting to have him? Did he think she was going to strip off her bra and fling it down the hatch and then throw herself topless into his waiting arms?

She was perspiring. The idea of going topless wasn't totally unappealing.

She stared at the aqua water, trying to decide how to handle this. Did she or did she not care if she made him mad? After all, he was enrolled in the Instituto where she taught. He might complain about her to the director.

Being a pretty redhead and a divorcée in Mexico was

downright dangerous. Men chased Vivian with more gusto than bulls charging a matador's red cape. Everywhere she went they ogled her, flirted with her, and made inappropriate remarks. And now…Aaron…even Aaron.

Did she give off a scent or what? They all thought she'd be an easy conquest. Was there a rule in the male mind that said once a woman had been initiated into the rite of sex, she had to have it? She needed a lover who saw her as nothing more than a piece of female meat, like she needed a hole in her head. Since her divorce, she'd said no to one and all, including her ex. Today wasn't going to be an exception.

She drew a tight breath and pressed her lips together as she studied the golden, bubbly liquid sparkling in the tropical sunlight. She was more disappointed in Aaron than she was angry. He was old enough to know better, and he was her best student. He loved diagraming grammar even more than she did. Until today he'd been a perfect gentleman. Maybe she should have known what he'd wanted even before he'd splashed all that champagne into her glass.

Still wondering what to do next, she glanced at her watch and was shocked that it was so late. Three o'clock. That got her going. She had to get her textbooks and leave. Unfortunately, they were down below on the bunk. Where *he* was.

Her former sister-in-law, Isabela, with whom she lived had given her a long to-do list this morning. Vivian had warned Isabela she had a Spanish lesson and might not get all the errands run, but she hadn't confessed she was driving all the way to Progreso for the lesson.

Vivian reviewed Isabela's list. She had to pick up the ironing and get home—fast.

The rigging sang in the warm sea breeze as Vivian leaned backward and flung the champagne into the water.

"What's taking you so long? Come on down," Aaron yelled from the cabin below.

"I have to go. Hand me my books."

"Come down and get them."

Before she could reply, her cell phone rang.

"Damn," he said. "Your in-laws, no doubt."

Nodding, Vivian smiled. The only two people who ever called her were Isabela or her brother, Vivian's own ex-husband, Julio, who still thought he could boss his ex around. Glad of an excuse to avoid a confrontation, Vivian grabbed her phone out of a bunch of tangled papers in her purse and answered it.

"You said you'd be here with the ironing an hour ago," Isabela said cheerfully. "The roofers…"

"I'm sorry, *querida*. Aaron's Spanish lesson ran a little longer than usual. I'm in Progreso. On his yacht."

"Don't you dare trust him if he has you on his yacht."

If there was one thing Isabela understood, it was the predatory male mind.

Vivian hung up smiling. Her sister-in-law was wonderful. She'd done so much for Vivian and her darling little son Miguelito since Vivian's divorce.

Even so, the one thing Vivian wanted more than anything was to leave Mexico and get her life back on track. She wanted to go back to college and become a certified teacher. She'd been too dependent on her wealthy sister-in-law's charity for too long, but Isabela always got so hurt when she said she wanted to return to the States, she hated to mention it.

"If you want your books, come on down," Aaron teased huskily.

Dreading dealing with Aaron, Vivian wiped her brow and scooted her bottom along the cockpit seat on her way to the hatch. The muggy air that stirred the turquoise waters felt hot, almost steamy. The sun set the tropical sky on fire. It was only April, and already the day was a scorcher. Thank goodness she was wearing shorts, and she was used to the heat.

Aaron shot her a challenging smile as he lifted her book satchel onto the counter beside the sink and dared her to come and get it. When she put her foot on the first step leading into the cabin, Aaron leaped toward her and tried to pull her down onto the bunk. Before she knew what had happened, she tumbled into his arms.

He laughed.

Regaining her balance, she jumped back and her hairpins scattered onto the flooring. Her red hair cascaded over her shoulders in waves of soft, bright silk.

"What do you think you're doing?" she sputtered.

"It's my turn to play teacher, Teacher," he whispered, moving so close, she felt his warm lips against her ear. "How about a little love lesson?"

"You drank too much champagne."

"Not really."

Aaron White was a retired doctor. He'd sailed to Mexico to enjoy the exotic locale and improve his Spanish. She gave him weekly Spanish lessons. As a change of pace this morning, because it had been sweltering in the city of Mérida where she lived and taught, she'd agreed to drive out to Progreso, which was on the coast, to have lunch and give him his lesson on his yacht.

Some lesson. All he'd wanted to do was guzzle champagne, sit too close to her and learn dirty words.

"Until today, I felt safe with you because you were a perfect gentleman," she said. When he kissed her cheek, she leaned against the wall and said, "I shouldn't have come here."

"What's wrong with enjoying yourself?"

She wasn't interested in Aaron. Not at all, but his holding her made her realize how long she'd done without a man's kisses or caresses. Or was it just the fierce, tropical heat that flooded her senses with sensual stirrings?

Her vulnerability frightened her. She *had* to get away.

When he tried to kiss her mouth, she twisted her head. Then he fingered the top button of her blouse, and she went rigid. Pushing his fingers away, she clenched her limp cotton collar against her throat.

"What's the matter?" he murmured.

"Everything." With a tight smile, she pushed him away.

"Relax. It's obvious it's been way too long since you got any…"

He touched the tip of her chin and she jumped away from him. "Who would have thought you'd look this hot with your hair down, when you're always so uptight and proper—"

Vivian gasped, feeling confused as she began scooping up hairpins off the sink and floor and re-pinning her hair into a prim little knot on the top of her head. "Don't you dare tell anybody at the Instituto about this."

"Or you might get fired?" He grinned at her, liking his power. "Calm down. I like the sexy divorcée better than the school teacher."

Her voice shook. "I—I need this job. I don't make much, but…"

"Relax."

When he slid a fingertip down her arm, her body went taut again and her breathing stopped.

"How long has it been since you've let a man touch you?"

She grabbed her books off the counter. "That is none of your business."

Aaron wasn't bad looking. Like her, he was a redhead, or he had been until a lot of the red had faded to silver. His eyes were blue, but not nearly such a brilliant shade of blue as hers. There were crow's feet beneath his eyes—he was, after all, thirty-one years older than she.

The humid heat was so stultifying in the cabin, she felt a little dazed as she began climbing the steps.

"Aaron, look, I ate too much, and you drank too much. Why don't we finish our Spanish lesson at the Instituto later this week?"

He laughed. "I liked our lesson today," he teased, grinning.

"I'm a single mom, Aaron. I have a little boy."

"Miguelito. Six years old. I've seen him at the Instituto. You're so cute I can tolerate one brat."

"He's not a brat. He's my darling little angel!" Miguelito had such a sunny disposition, he radiated love.

"In a few years you'll change your mind. I have three in college. Because of Miguelito, you didn't finish college, and you sacrificed seven years of your life down here as a glorified gofer for your in-laws."

"No." She could have gone back to the States, but the Escobars were the only family she had. Miguelito loved them. Her parents were dead and her dear uncle Morton had died, too, shortly after her marriage.

"They're using you."

"Isabela loves me."

"She's using you. That's why you have to sleep with me, so I'll fall in love with you and rescue you and your precious little Miguelito."

His remark annoyed her. "I want to be independent. I want to be a certified teacher."

"Teachers starve. A smart woman would at least consider…a doctor."

"You just want sex."

"Vivian, you can't hold what one rotten *manzana* did against all men," he said.

"It's not the *manzana* that terrifies me."

"I want to forget today," she said. "I'm sorry if by coming here I gave you the wrong idea."

"Or the *right* idea."

Before she could frame an adequate retort, her cell phone rang again.

"Which one of them is it this time?" Aaron demanded, just as Julio started yelling.

"Where are you, Vivi?"

She covered the mouthpiece. "It's Julio, if you must know. He wants to know where I am."

"Tell him it's none of his damn business. I'm sick and tired of him calling every time we have a lesson."

So was she…usually.

"Vivi, who are you talking to?" Julio demanded.

"I'm teaching a Spanish lesson. So I'm talking to Aaron, my student. On his boat."

"You're on his boat?" Julio's voice grew shrill. "Whatever you do, don't go below."

Vivian held the phone away from her ear until he was silent.

"You have no right to be jealous. You have a girlfriend…Tammy."

"The roofers are here," Julio said, his tone petulant. "Why aren't you?"

"They said they were coming two days ago," she replied. "They're here—now."

"Tell them the pool house is leaking to the left of the back door."

"Me? I'm here to visit my son. Eusebio didn't show up. Drunk again, I suppose, so Isabela needs somebody to drive her to the airport. You'd better hurry home. She's nearly ready to leave on this insane shopping trip. As if she needs clothes!"

Julio had a point. Isabela was flying to Houston to shop for clothes because a rich, famous architect named Cash McRay was flying in from London to visit her next week. She'd been writing him letters and dousing them with so much perfume that every time Vivian mailed one, her car reeked for hours.

"I can't deal with the roofers, watch Miguelito, and drive her to the airport, too," Julio said.

"I'm on my way," she replied, turning off her phone.

Like a lot of the men she knew down here, Julio was bossy, jealous, possessive, and totally helpless when it came to practical matters.

Divorce was the pits. Julio still thought he could run her

life. Worse, every time he got the chance, he tried to hit on her.

What she needed was stability. Why couldn't he just be a better, more consistent father?

She looked up at Aaron. "I have to get home now to see about Isabela's roofers and to drive her to the airport."

"Always errands for your spoiled sister-in-law."

"She's in love," said Vivian, her voice going dreamy. "That's a very special time in any woman's life."

"I hope she doesn't think she can manipulate him the way she does you."

"Look, I've gotta go—" Vivian hopped off his boat and raced toward her battered Chevy.

"Call me when you change your mind about sex, baby."

She got in and shut her door.

"A sexy woman like you can't do without it forever—"

She rolled her window up, hoping she wouldn't be able to hear him.

What is it about this testosterone-ridden country? She started her engine and drove off, leaving him in fumes of exhaust and plumes of dust.

She had to get her life back on track. Aaron White wasn't the answer. No man was.

There were some things, like making a life for herself, a real life, that a woman had to do on her own. Too bad it had taken her this long to figure that out.

Tires squealing, Vivian took the final turn on two wheels to her sister-in-law's sprawling, modern mansion with its shaded terraces and huge, airy rooms. The high walls surrounding the house were painted in bright Gauguin colors and had been a design of Isabela's world-famous father.

It was almost too late when Vivian saw the mound of orange fur in the middle of the road and hit her brakes. The dog lifted its head. His huge, brown eyes gave her a trusting stare.

Oh dear! "Concho! *Idioto!* Move!" Honking and swerving, she barely missed him.

The skinny orange dog had turned up in Isabela's wealthy neighborhood a week ago and instantly won Vivian's heart. At first Vivian had tried coaxing him out of the street. When that hadn't worked, she'd sprayed him with the hose every time she caught him, but, dumber than a zero, he still napped in the street every chance he got.

When Vivian parked her battered Chevy in the carport beside her sister-in-law's luxurious black, gold-trimmed Suburban, Concho trotted up, whining for a handout.

His velvet brown eyes got to her every time. Instantly, she began to dig in her purse for a treat. "All I've got is a sugar cookie."

He jumped, placing dusty paws on her thighs, and barked wildly, wolfing the cookie in a big gooey bite. She got out the sack of dog food she'd bought and filled his bowl in the carport and made sure he had water.

Usually Miguelito came running when he heard her muffler, but Julio was entertaining him today. It was early afternoon and so hot, Vivian unbuttoned the top two buttons of her white cotton blouse and fanned herself with her hand. When she headed through the wrought-iron gates, Concho whined.

She turned and petted him. "*Dios.* Be good. You know Isabela says no dogs behind the wall." Concho tilted his head and moaned when she abandoned him. "Gotta go see Isabel—now."

Concho's nails scraped concrete as he pranced back and forth. Then he hurled himself at the gate.

Out of the corner of her eye, Vivian saw Miguelito swimming in the pool. His dark face, so like his handsome father's, lit up when he saw her. The housekeeper sat by the pool watching him.

"Mommy, come swim!"

How he loved her, and he was such a little extrovert. He'd

grown up with so many relatives and friends lavishing love on him, he adored everybody.

Wishing she had time to play with him, she waved back. She could spend whole days just being with him. "I have to see *Tía*," she called.

Isabela opened the door of her balcony and called down to her. "Did you get the ironing?"

Vivian was nodding when she heard a wolf whistle. Instantly, she grabbed for the open plackets of her blouse. Looking around, she frowned when she spied Julio on the pool house roof with the roofer. Both men were shirtless and grinning at her like a pair of lusty apes.

Annoyed and more than a little mortified by their attentions, Vivian waved at Isabela and ran toward the house.

Racing lightly up the stairs with the ironing, Vivian found the door of Isabela's room standing open. Isabela was inside, looking gorgeous as usual. Her black hair was done in a sleek chignon and her dark eyes and face were aglow. The slim fit and bright color of her red slacks and matching silk blouse flattered her.

Two suitcases stood open on the bed and on the sumptuous, modern, stuffed chairs. Isabela snapped the locks of one of them and moved a suitcase to the floor so Vivian could set the laundry on the bed.

"I finally found those pictures I took of *him* in Mexico City," Isabela said as she rummaged through a second suitcase. "You've got to see them."

Ever since Isabela had come back from taking care of her father in Mexico City after he'd had a heart attack, she'd talked of nothing but Cash McRay.

"Your rich, famous architect from the United States?"

"Who else?"

Cash was the reason she was going to Houston to shop before he came for a visit. Apparently, seven walk-in closets full of couturier clothes weren't enough to assure success with this romance.

"When do you have to be at the airport?"

"There are the pictures of *him,*" Isabela said, handing Vivian a thick envelope as she fished in her purse for her plane tickets.

Isabela had been so flattering about him, Vivian didn't believe any man could be so wonderful. Even after all her pain with Julio, she could still remember how wonderful being in love had felt, and how blind a woman could be when under love's spell.

Faking a bored yawn, Vivian flipped through the pictures that were of the most arrestingly handsome man she'd ever seen—including Julio.

Cash McRay was tanned and big-framed and lean. His eyes were a deep, dark green, and something about them made her feel sad and a little lost…and way too vulnerable.

Her mouth went dry at the first photograph of him laughing with Isabel. The second was of him shirtless. At the sight of so much brown, sculpted muscle, Vivian's tongue stuck to the roof of her mouth. "Y-you look…er…great together."

She raced through the rest of the snapshots and placed them quickly on Isabela's bed.

Okay, so McRay was tall. So his body was rugged and rough-hewn. So his dark, brooding face was too like Julio's. *Dios!* So what?

So—she was breathless. So, she couldn't resist a second glance at the shots of him.

She picked the pictures up again. McRay's slashed cheekbones and that wide sensual mouth were so exquisite, Vivian's heart picked up its pace.

McRay looked as dark and strong as the stone faces carved on the Mayan ruins. He had an aquiline nose, a high forehead and thick, black brows. His hair was really extraordinary—thick and wavy and as lush and black as glossy sable where the ends grazed his collar.

"He has this thing about his hair," Isabela said. "He's very particular about who cuts it or touches it. He loves to have his head rubbed, too.''

Vivian's flesh tingled at the thought of running her hands through Isabela's modern-day Samson's pride and joy.

''Aren't his eyes gorgeous?'' Isabela whispered adoringly.

Every time Vivian glanced at McRay's dark green eyes, she felt a little breathless.

Carefully, she laid the pictures on Isabela's bed again. ''A man like that would never be faithful.''

''He was faithful to his first wife.''

''See—he's divorced. And...and nobody's as good as he looks.''

''Julio hurt you so much. Not everybody's Julio, you know,'' Isabela said softly, her eyes filled with sympathy.

''If McRay was so good to his first wife, why isn't he with her now?''

''What's gotten into you?''

''It's called divorce.''

''You're your biggest problem,'' Isabela said, but in a gentle tone. ''Not my brother, Julio. He didn't divorce you. You divorced him.''

''For a very good reason.''

''You have this bad attitude. In the beginning you love him madly—then you left him. Are all Americans like you?''

''Your brother cheated on me.''

''He is a man. You were his wife. He respected you. He still thinks of you as his wife.''

''It didn't feel like respect to me. I know I was at fault too. I—I believed in wild, true love back then, in two people destined for each other.''

''And now?''

''Julio taught me about real life.''

''He still wants you, you know.''

''And every other redhead he sees.''

''Just American redheads who are good in bed.''

"He shouldn't have told you how I was in bed! Sometimes I think he told every man in Mexico."

"Oh, *querida,* why can't you be happy here? We're your family. You're my sister." Isabela went to her and put her arms around her. "This is your country now. *Mi casa es tu casa.* My house is your house."

"But it isn't my house. And it won't ever be."

"It is if only you'd let it be." Isabela paused as if trying to think of a way to reach her. "You seem different today. Strange. Jumpy."

"I'm fine."

Isabela laughed softly. "Did Aaron make a pass at you?"

"I'd rather talk about your sex life—at least you have one. You don't need new clothes. Just get naked when you're alone with your Prince Charming," Vivian muttered in a grumpy tone.

"What a strange thing for you to say."

"I mean you don't need to go to Houston. Clothes are to impress other women."

Isabela tossed her glossy black head. "You Americans, especially you *gringas,* you think you are so smart. Cash is not like that."

"What is he like, then?" Vivian leaned forward, curious.

Hesitating, Isabela folded her sheerest negligee and placed it in her suitcase. "He lost his wife and daughter in a fire. His heart is shattered. He's not divorced. He didn't cheat."

"I shouldn't have said those things."

A lump formed in Vivian's throat and suddenly it was difficult to swallow. In a flash Vivian remembered the car accident that had devastated her. Her own parents, who'd been so in love and so much fun…her baby brother…everything she'd cherished gone in an instant.

Well-meaning relatives hadn't let her go to the funeral. The house had been filled with people who'd pampered her and made a fuss over her, but none of them had told her what was going to happen to her. There'd been some unspoken tension surrounding her future, for she was to live with her father's brother, Morton, and nobody thought he should have her except Vivian's mother and father, who were dead.

With an effort Vivian managed to push aside the scary memories of the loss she'd felt.

Against her better judgment, she frowned and lifted the photographs of the man Isabela was so set on catching, to review them a third time. As she sifted through them again, one by one, she felt sad for him, and, oh, how she wished she didn't. Not only did she see his pain, she felt it, lived it—and she became so charged by it, she had to blink her eyes because they filled with swift, hot tears.

How could she feel so connected to a total stranger? How could a few pictures of a man she'd never met make her feel so shaky and uncertain?

Maybe because she knew what it was to lose everything.

Slamming her last bag shut, Isabela announced she was packed and they'd better run if they were going to get to the airport on time. She took the stack of pictures from Vivian, removed one and stuck it in her purse, placing the rest in a drawer in her bedside table.

"Okay, let's go!" Isabela said as she glanced around the room. She rang a bell, and two male servants came to carry her luggage.

At the airport, Vivian hired porters and raced after Isabela when she ran inside the concourse. After Isabela had checked in and her bags had been searched and loaded on a conveyor belt, they hugged and said goodbye.

"Just call me on my cell when you get back and I'll be here in ten minutes," Vivian said.

"Promise?" Isabela kissed her cheek.

"Te prometo."

They hugged again and waved and then did it all over again. Vivian watched her until she disappeared around a corner.

As Vivian walked back out of the airport to the SUV, she

eyed the travel posters on the walls. If only she could just fly away as freely as Isabela and start a new life somewhere else—anywhere else.

She'd been so excited seven years ago when she'd come down here on an archaeological dig with her college class. She'd been eighteen and a virgin.

A week ago she'd had her twenty-fifth birthday.

She stepped out into the blazing, tropical sun and put her sunglasses on. The years would pass inexorably. If she didn't make some changes in her life and seize control, she *would* be here forever.

Three

Vivian took the stairs two at time and flung Isabela's bedroom door open. For a moment she thought the bedroom was empty. Then she saw eight suitcases lined up like soldiers beside the bed. The ninth lay open in the middle of the bed, new clothes spilling out of it.

But no Isabela.

Then Vivian heard somebody humming, and Isabela waltzed out of her closet in a sexy, black silk slip and bra that showed off her lush breasts and curvy hips. Ignoring Vivian, she went to her mirror and whirled playfully.

"Isabela—"

"Vivi!" Isabela lifted her eyebrows in feigned surprise. "Well...finally—I called and called you to come get me from the airport." Her black eyes flashed.

Vivian swallowed. "I—I know. The battery of my cell phone went dead. I was at the airport on time, though."

"When I couldn't reach you to tell you I was coming home on an earlier flight, I felt like a peon...standing on the curb, felt like an *idiota*…with all my suitcases. I called you at least ten more times.''

''I couldn't find the cord to charge my cell phone. I—''

''And Eusebio?''

''Sick.''

''If I find out he's home drunk again, I'm going to fire him this time.''

Vivian slid her sunglasses and keys into her purse and rushed to her sister-in-law. ''Please don't, and I promise…it won't ever happen again.''

Vivian steepled her fingers together and lowered her head in an attitude of repentance. ''I'm the most terrible sister-in-law in the whole world.''

Isabela smiled at her gently. ''I suppose anybody's battery could go dead…especially yours, since we call you so much.''

''I missed you calling me,'' Vivian whispered.

Isabela wrapped her arms around her and they hugged.

A few seconds later she let her go. ''I wish I had time to stay mad at you, but Cash is coming! And I don't know what to wear.''

''I told you before—nothing.''

''Stop with the jokes.'' Putting her hands on her small waist, Isabela smiled at her dazzling reflection and then at Vivian with obvious pride in her hourglass figure and cameo-perfect face.

Vivian flipped a red lock of hair out of her eyes and tried to act nonchalant. ''When will Prince Charming arrive?''

''He *is* Prince Charming. My very own Prince Charming.''

''I've never seen you like this. You're so in love.'' Warily Vivian eyed the drawer where Isabela had stashed her photographs of Cash. Vivian wasn't about to admit she'd snuck into Isabela's room several times to moon over those dumb pictures, and every time, she'd gotten that same vulnerable feeling in the pit of her stomach followed by a weird sense of connection to him.

''He's coming tonight.''

"What?"

Isabela whirled again. Her black eyes danced. "So, how do I look? I didn't eat a single french fry or chip in Houston."

"You know perfectly well how gorgeous you are. You appear transformed by love." Vivian's voice was dry.

Isabela arched a brow. "Transformed? Really?"

For the first time ever, Vivian felt a little jealous, not of Isabela's beauty but of her joyous self-confidence. Isabela was like a peacock, while Vivian had always been shy about her body and worn clothes that camouflaged her curves.

"Cash called me on my cell when I was in Houston...." Isabela rattled on about the phone call, repeating everything he'd said. "He wants to see the beach house. You see, he's agreed to help me repair it and enlarge it. He doesn't know that I intend to turn it into our very own paradise."

"Where you'll both live happily ever after?"

"If tonight goes well—" Isabela paused "—we'll drive out there tomorrow."

The beach house was located on a sugary strip of beach in the nearby fishing village and port of Progreso, the same town where Aaron kept his boat. The house had suffered extensive damage during a recent hurricane. Thus, it was now a magnificent ruin with all its windows and doors boarded.

"We can swim and enjoy the grounds and picnic. He can sketch," Isabela said.

Vivian was forming a romantic picture of them there when Miguelito squealed beneath them in the walled yard. Rushing to the glass door that opened onto a balcony, she stared down at her son. He was walking hand in hand with Julio and Tammy toward the pool, smiling up at them lovingly, the way he did at everybody...smiling as if he were *their* little boy.

Vivian wanted him to love everybody. Still, she pressed her fingertips to the glass and emitted a little sigh.

Divorce—would it ever stop hurting? She still felt guilty about leaving Julio, about them not being a family. She'd been too young to marry, not that she regretted Miguelito.

Julio was carrying a yellow beach ball. Golden-skinned Tammy, who was barely eighteen, looked sleek and sexy in a white thong bikini.

Just like I did…seven years ago….

Tammy was an American student at the Instituto. She'd come to the Yucatán to study the ruins and improve her Spanish. Unlike most of Julio's girlfriends, Tammy loved kids, and Miguelito enjoyed her.

Which was good.

So why did her heart ache as she circled herself with her arms and squeezed herself hard? Ever since her parents and little brother died, all she'd wanted was to be part of a happy family.

"What's so interesting down there?" Isabela glided soundlessly across the room and joined her at the window.

"Do you think he misses his real mommy at all?" Vivian whispered in a low, raw tone.

Tammy squealed when Miguelito splashed her, and Julio pulled Tammy away from the boy, circling her with his bronzed arms. He gave her a kiss. The girl wrapped her legs exuberantly around Julio while Miguelito watched them spellbound.

Vivian's fingernails raked the warm glass.

"Now, don't get upset," Isabela said. "You don't want Julio for yourself, and you know he can't exist without a girlfriend."

"Even when I was pregnant. If I don't get Miguelito out of this country fast, he'll wind up just like his daddy, and history will repeat itself."

"Julio is a wonderful father."

"But not a wonderful husband. I don't want Miguelito to see women, especially young pretty ones, only as sex objects, and other women as servants."

"You worry too much," Isabela said with a soft laugh.

"I'm afraid I have very different views than you about sex and love."

"Do you? Sometimes I wonder."

"You are more than just a beauty. You have a mind."

"I'm smart enough not to try to compete with men, if that's what you mean."

"It isn't." Vivian pounded on the glass to distract Miguelito from the fused pair, who were still engaged in an endless, torrid series of kisses.

Tammy saw her first and shyly pushed against Julio's brown shoulder and waved up at her. Then father and son waved sheepishly too.

"Well, I hope you're happy now." Amusement glimmered in Isabela's slanting dark eyes. "You sure broke them up."

"You just don't want me to spoil your mood."

"Exactly. I'm in love."

"With love."

"With Cash. He was so shy on the phone. I'm almost sure he's coming here to propose."

"You don't know? Why, Isabela, sex-goddess extraordinaire, you're losing your touch."

"Don't tease me. Not about him. And if he does ask me, I'll throw a huge dance to announce our engagement. We've got to act surprised, but we've got to be ready, too. So you've got to help me."

"Of course, *querida.* Anything."

"We've got to get the house and the guest room, everything into top shape. I told the servants when I got in."

"I noticed the kitchen was in an uproar." A pause, and then it occurred to Vivian how terrible life would be here without Isabela. She swallowed. "If you marry him, where will you two live?"

"San Francisco. Of course, Cash travels all over the world. Just like Papá."

"If you leave, I'll miss you...."

Their glances met. Vivian struggled to hide the desperate sense of loss and abandonment that was a legacy of being orphaned at an early age.

Isabela clapped her hands and moved closer, holding out her arms. "You are always teasing me and complaining—but you do love me. You do. Like a sister."

"You're the only family…"

The passionate Isabela enfolded her in a touching embrace and squeezed her waist tightly. For an instant Vivian's eyes stung with hot wetness.

"Silly, *preciosa,* you and Miguelito will come with me. *Por supuesto, ven conmigo.*"

"But—"

"Don't cry!"

"Don't be ridiculous! I'm not!" But her eyes burned, and her heart beat in painful, jerky strokes.

"Your eyes are as bright as cherries. Don't you know, I can't live in the States—not without family. You are my sister. We will find you a little house near ours. You will help me catch him—yes?"

"You're taking me with you?" Vivian dabbed at her eyes. She couldn't believe Isabela's generous offer.

She and Miguelito might go home.

"You've told me you want to go back to school and that there's no opportunity here. This is *our* chance. If you help me, we will both realize our dreams."

"I—I can't believe you'd take—"

"Believe it. All you have to do is play fairy godmother and help me catch my prince."

"But you are so beautiful. How could I possibly help?"

"I don't understand you Americans, and when he arrives, he must have the most wonderful time of his life. Everything must be perfect. You say I am beautiful, but you don't understand who he is. He is like a god. He could have any woman. And like you say, he is used to women who aren't afraid to reveal they have minds."

Vivian had never seen Isabela so filled with self-doubt, and because of her own self-doubts, she sympathized.

"He is like royalty…an international celebrity in his own

right. He is not in love with me—yet. He is still in love with *her,* his first wife. He never talks about it, but I can sense the way he feels. He can look so dark, so sad, and his eyes can look so empty.''

Vivian's heart beat uneasily. She had felt what he felt too— just from looking at his photograph. ''I know what you mean,'' she said softly.

''If I'm lucky, he'll pop the question tonight, first thing. But until he does…''

Vivian shivered a little. ''I'll prepare the guest room for him,'' she said, suddenly eager to end this discussion about Isabela's Prince Charming.

When she left Isabela, she knew she had to forget Cash McRay's green eyes and that strange feeling of sorrow and connection she felt toward him. She loved Isabela like a sister. Her loyalty was to Isabela.

The best way to quit fantasizing about a man who'd lost the woman he'd loved and wore his grief in his pain-ravaged eyes was to work hard. Vivian marched down to the kitchen and made long lists for the servants. Next she took two maids to Cash's guest room and listed what needed to be done. As she was leaving, Vivian spotted a puddle on the bathroom floor near the water heater. When she turned the hot water heater on, water spewed out of a broken pipe, showering her.

She screamed, and the maids doubled over with laughter. Then she started laughing too. Finally, she turned the water off, but a look at herself in the mirror brought more giggles. Dripping wet, her bright hair glued to her scalp, Vivian looked like a giant, drowned rat.

Still laughing, she went to the garage to tell Rodrigo. Then she returned to Isabela's bedroom to check in with Isabela, who laughed at her too.

''Cash just called. You'll have to change at once and repair your hair. His plane is on the ground.''

''I'm too tired. I'm going to shower and go to bed.''

"But I want you to meet Cash."

"In the morning."

"But, you said you'd help—"

"He's an American. With an American man, you put romancing him first and family second. It's important that you don't overpower him. Trust me on this."

Isabela hugged her until she was as soaked as Vivian. "All right. Tonight we'll have a candlelight dinner by the pool, just the two of us. Lots of candles. And I'll wear this." She lifted a sexy red sheath from her bed. "How are these for glass slippers?"

The shoes, although made of plastic, did indeed look like glass slippers adorned with thousands of sparkling red stars.

"You will be the most perfect Cinderella ever."

An hour later, when Vivian was upstairs alone in her bedroom, with her stringy, wet hair and her sunburned face, she sensed *him* even before the outer door slammed and he entered the walled courtyard.

One minute she was fine. Then it was as if her world shifted crazily on its axis. The air was suddenly so dense and hot she could barely breathe.

More doors banged. A dog's claws scraped tile. The animal began barking inside the courtyard. Isabela didn't allow dogs.

The mutt yapped again.

Curious, Vivian stepped out onto her balcony, and a man's deep, pleasant voice from the patio below made her quiver and slink into the shadows of the ancient pomegranate tree.

"Anyone can see the mutt's half starved, Isabela. Indulge me," the voice said.

"You can't adopt every mangy dog in Mexico."

Isabela moved toward him, hips undulating. He gulped his entire glass of wine and backed away from her.

"My cabdriver nearly hit him."

"Because he's so stupid he sleeps in the middle of the street."

"Just look into his eyes. What soul!"

"Oh, my God, Cash—he's already eaten half our grilled chicken dinner."

"We won't starve, Isabela. Do you have soap and a hose? As soon as he eats, I'll bathe him."

"Surely one of the servants can deal with him. You've come such a long way. Why don't we enjoy each other?"

Again he backed away from her. "If you don't mind, I'd prefer to bathe him myself." The beautiful voice was harder, crisper. "You can watch...if you'd enjoy that."

Fisting her hands, Vivian stirred restlessly. She felt strangely possessive and jealous of Concho. Why had Cash McRay fixed on *her* skinny, orange stray? The last thing she needed was to feel another connection to the man.

As if the dog sensed her, Concho trotted to the patio under her balcony, looked up and began to whine. When Cash followed, Vivian whirled inside and eased her glass door shut. Trying not to think about the couple outside, she peeled off her wet clothes, bathed, and washed her hair, standing in the warm shower far longer than was necessary, as if to wash the memory of Cash's voice and presence from her consciousness. Finally, she slipped on a cotton nightgown and towel-dried her hair.

She'd missed her swim this morning and now again tonight. Maybe that was partly why she felt so strange and restless as she moved about her bedroom straightening shelves and drawers that were perfectly straight already.

Miguelito was still with Tammy and Julio, or she would have gone to his room and played games or read books with him. When she tried to read in bed, her mind was too scattered to concentrate. So, she got up again and paced.

If only she could swim, but she couldn't. Not with Isabela entertaining Cash down by the pool.

Tonight was too important—maybe he'd propose. She had to stay focused on the fact that he was her ticket to a new life.

When Vivian lay down on her bed a long while later, she

felt exhausted, but too confused to sleep. She kept thinking about Concho and the fact that Cash cared about *her* dog. The feeling that they were connected in some mysterious way intensified.

It's been too long since you got any...

She wished Aaron hadn't said that. She wished the mattress wasn't so soft. She balled the sheets in her hands and tried to lie still.

Why couldn't she sleep? Why was she dwelling on this fantasy about a man she didn't even know? Worse—he was Isabela's, and she adored Isabela.

Finally Vivian got up, opened the door and padded barefoot out onto her shadowy balcony again. The sultry night air smelled of mango and avocado, and of grilled chicken and garlic.

Hundreds of candles lit up the pool area. She could see the lovers from her balcony. Isabela pranced about under the ancient pomegranate tree in her sexy, strapless red dress that was the exact shade of the walls and her strappy, see-through heels, while Cash kept moving out of her range.

Mostly Vivian watched Cash, who was half hidden by the tropical foliage. He was big and virile looking in jeans and boots. He was whipcord lean and had the tight-hipped swagger of a street fighter, and yet he was, apparently, a highly sophisticated, brilliant man.

Vivian found that she liked watching him move. His big, raw-boned body somehow went with his rough, haunted face.

Concho liked him too. Claws clicking, the dog padded after him everywhere, and when Cash's brown hand fell to his side, the mutt's head was there to lick his fingers and be stroked. Cash seemed much more comfortable with the dog than he did with Isabela.

Don't try so hard, Isabela.

Still, Isabela would win. She always did. Broken-hearted or not, the rugged Cash McRay, who had a soft spot for mongrels, didn't stand a chance against the seductive, fiery Isabela.

And I want Isabela to win. I do.

Remembering how gently Julio had courted her with candlelit dinners and dances, Vivian knew McRay was in over his head. Julio specialized in reluctant virgins, just as Isabela specialized in wounded rich men.

And Isabela had broken too many hearts to count. Not that Isabela kept a list of conquests or heartbreaks. She was resilient and optimistic. In her mind, the present man was the only one.

If Isabela pulled this off, Vivian would get to go home to the States. But oddly, Vivian wanted Cash to find true love and be happy and not simply be swept away.

Suddenly Concho left Cash's side and trotted over to stand underneath Vivian's balcony. He lifted his head and began to bark excitedly as if she were a skunk or a raccoon he'd treed.

"Go away! Git!" Vivian whispered.

At the sound of her voice, Concho leaped against the pomegranate tree and howled. When Vivian heard a man's footsteps, she quickly shrank deeper into the shadows.

"What's wrong, Spot?"

Spot! Spot? Concho didn't have a spot on him.

Cash was underneath her too now. Vivian barely dared to breathe when he planted two large, broad feet squarely underneath her balcony.

"Somebody up there, Spot? A cat, maybe?"

Vivian's heart knocked. *Just me.*

She *felt* him, and she knew he felt her. Because he stayed there, even after Isabela called to him.

Some weird, out-of-body chemistry was definitely going on. The air grew colder and seemed to snap as if it were as charged with electricity as air after a summer storm. The leaves of the pomegranate stirred, as did the tendrils along Vivian's nape.

Vivian wrapped her arms around herself tightly and clamped her teeth together to keep them from chattering.

"Somebody up there?" he repeated, his deep voice silky and seductive.

"That's Vivian's bedroom," Isabela told him. "She's asleep."

No, she's biting her lips until they bleed and trembling like a crazy woman while wave after wave of wanton heat washes over her.

Oh dear, if this mad feeling didn't stop soon, she was sure she'd melt and become a puddle.

"Go away," she whispered, her legs turning to jelly as she sank against the wall. "Please, both of you—just go away."

"Vivian?" he whispered into the still night air. "Are you up there?"

Four

—————

Vivian woke up on a shudder of longing to a giant tropical moon flooding her bedroom with magical white light. Slowly she became aware of her hot flesh tingling.

She licked her lips. Half awake, and breathless from her dream, she scrambled into her bathrobe and dashed to her balcony, where she stared at the moon and tried her best to forget her outrageous fantasy. But the harder she tried to forget him, the more indelibly he became engraved on her mind.

She'd been dreaming she was naked and sitting on a broad, virile Cash McRay, who was as naked as the day he was born. He'd been solid and warm, sculpted of muscle. His eyes had burned green and bright with tenderness and desire, and even now, just remembering, her body thrummed with longing.

She could still hear his voice. *"Vivian? Are you up there?"*

With shaking fingers Vivian wrapped the thick folds of her robe up high under her throat the way a prim old maid might. But she wasn't an old maid. She was a divorcée. For the first time, she was fulfilling all her suitors' fantasies about her.

Aaron's words returned to haunt her. *"It's obvious it's been too long…"*

To get her mind off the possibility of sex with Isabela's beloved, Vivian decided to go for a swim.

A swim—the mere thought energized her and had her racing to her bureau and rummaging through a drawer for her red bikini. Even before she shook out the drawer onto a floor already teeming with clothes she hadn't hung up for the past few days, she remembered she'd left it in the pool house bathroom.

Five minutes later she was there, tearing her cotton gown and bathrobe off as if demons possessed her.

She couldn't believe she'd dreamed that she'd spent half the night on top of Isabela's future husband, her mouth and tongue running wild over his wide brown chest and throat. He'd hauled her closer, so close she'd felt his hardness against her pelvis. Just the memory made her toes curl against the tile floor.

Vivian wasn't good at hiding her feelings—a major flaw—especially when she had a guilty conscience. She'd die of mortification if she blushed and simpered like a schoolgirl with her first crush when Isabela introduced them at breakfast.

Isabela trusted her.

Just thinking about the way his lips had caressed every part of her body made her cringe. Even so, she imagined it all again…

She had to get a grip, to clear her mind of such treacherous, misplaced longings. She didn't even know him!

It was beautiful outside—the stars bright against an ink-dark sky. Vivian gazed out the window at the Big Dipper and then the North Star. If the days in Mérida broiled a person, April nights were romantically lush and sweet-scented.

She knew her way around the dark bathroom, so she didn't bother to turn on the light, not even when she heard a sound from the next room. Then she groped for her bathing suit, which should have been hanging from the towel rack by the tub. Only when it wasn't there did she flip on the light to look for it. Seven gilded mirrors—Isabela went in for overstated opulence—lit and reflected every inch of Vivian's soft, creamy skin. Her red hair was tousled and fell about her shoulders.

Momentarily blinded, she shielded her eyes with her hand while they adjusted to the glare. Quickly she lowered the window shade. She moved languidly, at ease with her seven reflections even though she was naked—until she removed her hand from the light switch and fumbled on the counter for her bikini. Her brain didn't register what her eyes saw for a second or two.

Her bikini wasn't there.

She squinted, focusing on a scarred leather bag with the initials *C.M.* carved in the middle. It was a man's expensive suitcase, and it had no business lying closed on that luggage rack with an expensive pair of black silk slacks dripping out of it.

On the white tile counter, a man's electric razor was plugged into a wall socket. Her eyes darted to the bottle of aftershave and the squashed tube of toothpaste right beside it. Last of all she saw the bra of her red bikini stuffed in a far corner behind Isabela's bronze flamingos.

She was reaching for her bikini when a deep, throaty voice that was rough with sleep came from the direction of the sofa bed near the pool table.

"Wow! Who the hell are you—Sleeping Beauty?" The man's heavy breathing seemed to grow more ragged on every word he uttered.

Don't, please, don't you dare be Cash McRay!

Of course he was Cash.

She knew who he was even though her desperate mind fought to deny it. His sexy passionate voice turned her to mush.

Concho yawned sleepily. Paws crossed under his wet nose,

the canine ingrate was curled up at the end of Cash's sofa bed as if he belonged there.

Her nipples went as hard as rubies. All she had to do was take a flying leap into that bed to make her dream come true.

Isabela… This isn't happening.

Suddenly Vivian was trembling and digging her nails into her palms. Next, she was jabbing frantically at the light switch.

"So, you're the girl who goes with the itty-bitty, red bikini? You're taller than I pictured you. Bigger at the top, too."

When she missed the switch on the first try, she cried out in sheer frustration.

He laughed. "I was having a nightmare when you barged into my dreams."

"You too?" Her glance shot toward him and her skinny dog.

Half covered in the sheet, Cash looked long and sleek and brown, and very masculine. His shoulders were wide, his chest matted with dark hair.

Her mouth went dry, but she got wet in other places. Suddenly, it was all she could do to remember to breathe, much less act like any normal, modest, *sensible* young woman, who found herself *naked* in a complete stranger's bedroom in the middle of the night.

As she stood there, seconds ticked by—as if she were paralyzed or hypnotized.

"This weird barber had me tied to his chair" came that deep beautiful voice from the bed.

"What are you talking about?" she whispered.

"I dreamed about a crazy barber."

"I don't want to hear this."

"I told him not to cut much of my hair off, but he had an electric razor, and he'd already taken a swipe at my scalp. 'Oops,' he said. I wanted to kill him, but it was a dream, so I just lay there."

Like I'm just standing here—as if this is a dream and I'll wake up and everything will be back to normal.

"Then he put a bowl on my head and began to shave the hair off around my ears and neckline."

Turn off the light, dummy.

Vivian clamped down on her tongue with her teeth. The coppery flavor of blood and the shooting pain brought her to her senses. Quick as a flash, she hit the switch, and the room went mercifully black.

"Forget you ever saw me," she mumbled, her hot body sagging against the cool tiled wall because her legs had turned to jelly.

"You must be the sister-in-law," he murmured dryly. "The one who didn't want to meet me."

"No! I'm not her! And I don't know her. And you don't either," she replied, panicked.

English. He was speaking English. Real American English. She loved to hear Americans talking in the street because the sound of her native tongue with its flat vowels reminded her of home. Just the sound of his voice made her long for a normal life with a purpose and a future.

Just the sound of it made her body heat and throb and her heart long for her wanton dream to come true.

"What do you think my dream meant?" he asked conversationally.

She could hear every raspy breath she took. "I—I don't care! It was a ridiculous dream!"

"Not to me. I'm most particular about letting some freak mess with my hair. It means something. Trust me."

"Look! I just had a nightmare myself—and it meant nothing!" She spoke in a frantic whisper as she moved away from the wall and began to fumble in the dark for her bathrobe, cursing when her fingers were shaking too violently to pull it on. "Damn!"

"Tell me your dream, and I'll tell you what it meant," he offered.

"I don't think so."

"Trust me, I'm good at this," he said.

She almost moaned.

Bed sheets rustled. Not good. "You stay right where you are!" she screeched, backing toward the shower, stumbling over two objects that felt like a pair of large shoes.

"I liked the light on," he said. "The view was better."

"Well, I don't. And I don't want to know who you are. Or hear about your hair. I want to forget I ever met you—"

Liar. She wanted to lick his long, lean body, to taste him. No. That was a dream.

"The name's Cash. Cash McRay. And I damn sure want to know the name of the naked lady who saved me from a fiend with hair clippers. I was drenched in sweat from terror— and then there you were, like Venus arising from the sea to rescue me. Exquisite Aphrodite."

She groaned aloud. She'd dreamed about getting naked on top of him. Now her future brother-in-law had seen her in her birthday suit and was waxing poetic. Her heart was racing.

"We are not part of some myth!" she snapped.

"You gonna tell me about your dream?"

Why didn't men ever, just once, do what they were supposed to do? "Why aren't you in the guest suite where you belong? Or better yet, in Isabela's bed?"

"Maybe you're my destiny."

"Don't be ridiculous."

"You did appear to save me from that mad barber."

His laughter brought fresh panic. She put her arm through the wrong hole of her bathrobe. Next she got all tangled up in the sash. She stumbled on the folds of the robe.

Then somehow, miraculously, she quit tripping over the garment, stabbed her arms through the proper holes and wrapped the robe around herself as if it were a shroud. Breathlessly, her chest heaving, tender pointed nipples mashing against terry cloth so hard they hurt, she tied the sash in a tight knot.

"Broken pipe in the bathroom. No water. Besides, I kind of like it out here," he said.

She almost hated him more because his answer was so reasonable.

"Did you see me—"

He laughed again. "Everything. Seven extra you's are imprinted on my male brain forever—Aphrodite."

"Just be quiet and go back to sleep and dream about that barber."

"Do you want to go back to sleep and dream your dream—"

Dear God.

"See this," he continued, "you're way more fun. Not that I'm going to let you near hair clippers in your present mood. My whole body's buzzing—terror from the barber and then sensory overload from you. I needed to get up early and read architectural journals. But, hey, if you're going skinny-dipping, I'll join you—Aphrodite."

"No—"

"Isabela said she'd introduce us at breakfast."

"I have an errand downtown."

"Join us for lunch, then? By the pool maybe?"

"No! I'll be gone all day. Teaching."

"Aaron White by chance? He called you last night. Said it was urgent. Said he couldn't wait to finish his lesson. What exactly are you teaching him?"

"I'm not in the mood for this conversation. Surely you can understand—"

"Look, I'm sorry I teased you a while ago. I mean, it's not every day a naked goddess wakes me up. Let's be reasonable—"

"No! *You* look. I'm the last thing from reasonable!"

"That's exactly what Isabela said."

"She told you about me?"

"She adores you. And your son. Miguelito, I believe?"

"Then I'll never be able to face you."

"Why not? You're beautiful. Surely you know you have nothing to be ashamed of. I'm an architect. I appreciate beauty. I just got back from Florence. I looked at lots of naked ladies in paintings. Naked statues, too."

"I'm not some statue or painting. No man has seen me like this…. Not since my divorce," she whispered. "Oh God. Forget I said that. My sex life is none of your business."

"Hey, don't be embarrassed." His voice was beguilingly gentle now. "Okay, why don't we just pretend this never happened."

"Because you're a man, and men always take advantage—"

"You've been in Mexico way too long."

"You're right about that."

He laughed. "I know how to fix this."

Before she could say anything, he jumped out of bed and tugged at the chain on the lamp, flooding the room with light. Faster than she could blink, he ripped off the sheet wrapped around his lean waist and exposed himself to her.

"Oh my God! Oh—"

He was huge—everywhere.

She tried to stare at the sheet on the floor, but the temptation of a fully aroused naked man, after so long…

Inch by inch, her eyes climbed his long, powerful, tanned legs. His hips were lean, his belly washboard flat. Other parts met with her approval, too. And, of course, she stared at the one thing she shouldn't have looked at.

He smiled with immense male satisfaction when she finally met his gaze. "There! You've viewed the family jewels! We're even!"

Even as she gaped, she blushed furiously. "You're crazy. And you make me crazy. Do you know that?"

"Is that why your eyes are bugging and your lower jaw's

hanging open?'' He laughed. ''Has it been that long since you saw a naked man? Or are you that impressed?''

Her breathing was choppy. She shut her eyes for a second and clamped her mouth shut. ''You're unbearably...conceited...sex-crazed.''

''Do go on.'' His voice was no more than a throaty whisper.

He tensed, stretching his lean, dark frame like a giant cat. She watched his muscles flex and contract with unwanted fascination—and a pure unadulterated female admiration that made her body feel molten. Yes! He was overwhelmingly masculine.

Dios. Women weren't supposed to care about size, but she wasn't displeased at the way he looked. Big men, big hands, big... Big. Period. Okay, so she wasn't politically correct, big turned her on.

Somehow he took up way more space than he physically occupied. Then he grinned, and she really felt bowled over.

She fought not to stare down there again—fought and failed. His aura of virility filled the room, hotly flooding her senses and making every nerve ending buzz.

Somewhere she'd heard you had to get crazy people and criminals talking.

''Oh my God. I can't believe... You're naked.'' Her voice was squeaky. She sounded like a mouse.

''Big deal.'' His voice hadn't changed a bit. ''I said we're even a while ago. Relax.''

''Relax?'' Someone else had used that word recently.

Her shaking hand went to her throat where she could feel her rapid pulse. ''Right, relax,'' she said in her mouse's voice. ''Relax—with you naked.''

His hard face softened as he took a step toward her.

She jumped a foot and then scooted backward fast, bruising her big toe when she slipped and stumbled over a pair of shoes.

"Don't you dare take another step toward me. Don't you dare try to touch—"

His white grin widened. "I think you want me to touch you. And I will…if you invite me to."

"No. No!"

Then he pointed to the floor at a puddle of blue denim. "Can I get dressed now?"

Somehow she made her head bob her assent despite acute disappointment.

He leaned down and scooped up a pair of jeans. Then he stepped into them, slowly, one long, lanky leg at a time. She watched, mesmerized.

He zipped his jeans, slowly, oh, so slowly, careful not to catch anything important. "There. Feel all better now? I saw you. You saw me. Now we can move on."

Maybe he could move on, but she was stuck. She kept seeing his big brown body. She couldn't get him or that image out of her mind.

Her skin felt as hot as fire. Her heart was still tripping over itself. "Th-this didn't happen."

His green eyes drilled her. "Yeah, it did. And for me, it was a life-changing moment."

"I was never here."

"We got naked together, Vivian. And it was fun. The most fun I've had—"

He stopped, and she saw the pain in his eyes. He'd lost his wife and his little girl. She didn't want to remember anything that made him seem more human and real.

"I didn't have fun," she insisted.

He grinned, a lopsided, charming grin. His black eyebrows quirked above his beautiful eyes. And his pain that made her feel so vulnerable vanished.

"Right."

"Whatever you do, don't you dare tell Isabela about this. I love her. She's like a sister. I can't be here with you…like this."

"What do you take me for?"

"Women down here are insanely jealous," she said as she moved toward the door.

"Can I hope she has something to be jealous about?" he whispered, his eyes going so deep and dark, she shivered.

"What?"

"I told you—for me this was a life-changing moment."

When he didn't look away, she was aware of something hot and dangerous filling the air. He wanted her. He didn't want to let this go any more than she did.

But she loved Isabela.

"No," she whispered. "You have to get over it. We have to forget it. For *her* sake."

"What a shame," he said at last, but he continued to study her. "Okay. Then it was a dream, and we both woke up. Okay. Your secret is safe with me."

Vivian dashed for the door. "No way, not in a million years, can I meet your eyes over breakfast—not with Isabela watching! I'll feel like I betrayed her."

"You didn't. We didn't do anything."

Yet. "Look, I've gotta go!"

"Sweet dreams," he whispered. "Which reminds me—you never did tell me your dream."

"Don't hold your breath." She flung the door wide.

"I got naked for you."

"And that was such a huge sacrifice for you, I'm sure." She licked her lips. "You were showing off."

He beamed. "Must've been some dream," he said, "to get you down here in the middle of the night anxious for a chilly swim. Knowing you, it had to be about sex."

"You don't know me!"

"Did you dream about sex or not?"

Heat washed her neck and face.

When he laughed, she ran before he could ask any more questions.

"Don't let anybody see you in that bathrobe. It's inside out," he yelled.

Five

Cash slammed the pool house door behind him and squinted in the brilliant sunshine. He felt disoriented and not himself.

He'd just gotten off the phone with Isabela. He didn't want to think about why he'd deliberately put the engagement ring back in his suitcase and left it in the pool house, when only yesterday he'd been so sure about the new direction he wanted his life to take.

And after Aphrodite, Cash was in no mood to share another meal on the patio with the vivacious, super-sexy Isabela, but she had already called him twice.

"Your *huevos motuleros* are nearly ready," she'd murmured.

"You remembered." He'd developed an enthusiasm for Marco's favorite breakfast when they'd brought Marco home from the hospital the last time they'd all been together.

"I remember everything we did in the city and everything we said." When she paused, he heard her breathing. "I can't wait to see you."

"Likewise."

"Likewise?" She'd sounded confused.

"It's an American expression."

"Not a very romantic one—"

He'd hung up on her too abruptly. He was blowing it.

Damn you, Aphrodite! You're the wild card thrown down onto green felt after I've already played a good hand very badly.

Isabela was perfect for him. He rubbed his temples and squinted again. The bright light, the drone of the bees buzzing in the purple bougainvillea that dripped from the roof, the red and blue walls, the vivid green lawn—all set a million little hammers pounding painfully in his brain.

Every time Isabela had come on to him last night, he'd swigged down more alcohol, until he'd barely been able to stagger to bed. He now had the hangover from hell.

He was smoothing his white collar down and sliding his Ray-Bans on when the dark, skinny kid he'd seen playing soccer outside with a maid and a gardener earlier grinned from ear to ear and shouted to him.

"Hola! Señor—" The kid grinned again.

The smile softened something inside Cash, and he went instantly on full alert. Usually he avoided kids, especially extraordinarily appealing ones like this one, because they made him think about Sophie.

"Hola," he said, striding even faster as he headed for the patio at the far edge of the spacious lawn. Spot trotted along after him.

The kid switched to English. "Have you seen my mommy?"

The question stopped Cash cold. The vision of those sweet, young curves he'd longed to touch and taste and smell played like a rerun in his mind. Aphrodite's body and those tangles of liquid copper curls flowing over her shoulders would doubtlessly be imprinted forever in some deep, primal part of his male brain. Again he saw her ruby-red nipples, her swollen breasts, her flushed cheeks, her long-lashed, blue eyes. Most of all he remembered the longing in her eyes.

When Cash didn't answer, the kid grinned again and lowered his voice to a plaintive stage whisper. "She's not upstairs. She's not anywhere. And I'm scared of the bees."

Alarm flashed through Cash. "She has to be somewhere."

"She keeps her bathing suit in the pool house. I thought maybe she'd gone there looking for it or something."

Cash felt a wave of heat flash beneath his collar. "Haven't seen her...er...lately—"

"Usually she swims with me or watches me swim."

"She likes to swim, does she?" Cash replied, moving again, away from the pool because the kid was staring at his face with laser-bright eyes and smiling that smile that cut through all his defenses.

"Do you have a kid?"

"What?" Cash turned, feeling trapped.

The boy's expression was eager, rapt.

"A little girl," Cash admitted.

"Why isn't she with you?"

The muscles in his shoulders bunched. "She...couldn't come...." Cash felt numb, dead in the center. He should run. He stood where he was—paralyzed.

"Oh." There was a pause, and the boy's smile faltered. "Are you divorced?"

"No."

The maid and the gardener sitting in lawn chairs on the opposite side of the pool were watching them curiously.

"What's her name?" the boy said.

"Who?"

"Your kid."

Cash's lips barely moved. "Sophie."

"Mine's Miguelito, and my mommy takes me everywhere."

"Except not this morning," Cash said, hoping to end this impossible conversation.

Miguelito's mouth puckered. "So will you watch me swim till she comes?"

"You have people watching you already—"

"Pedro and Lisa," the kid said, waving to them and yet never taking his eager eyes off Cash.

The servants waved back reassuringly. When the kid's black eyes, eyes too like Isabela's, continued to drill him pleadingly, Cash felt even more trapped, just like he had last night by the kid's aunt. The Escobars came on too strong.

"I want you because I'm scared of the bees," Miguelito said simply but in that engaging child's whisper that made Cash feel big and important.

"Bees?" he asked, remembering the droning.

"They keep drinking out of the pool. One stung me yesterday." He pointed to his shoulder.

"Your shoulder looks okay to me."

"There's a little red dot where it bit me."

"You know you're a lot bigger than a bee."

"But it really hurts." Miguelito glanced worriedly at the bougainvillea. "Stay—please."

Much to his surprise, Cash stalked to the pool and sat down. The kid grinned, and Spot came up and lay down beside Cash.

He was *her* kid. He was cute and friendly, maybe too friendly, but he made Cash feel needed…just as Sophie used to. Maybe he could do this.

Grinning again, his dark eyes flashing with self-importance now that he'd increased his admiring audience, Miguelito climbed out of the pool, and then ran, spattering water all over the red tiles.

"No corras," the maid screamed when his small, wet feet slid out from under him and he nearly fell.

Miguelito slowed for a second, regained his balance, shot Cash another big grin and then sped up again. He leaped up the chrome stairs to the diving board as agilely as a baby monkey. "Watch me dive, *señor!*" Fearlessly he jumped up and down at the end of the board. "Can your little girl dive?"

Sophie hadn't lived long enough to learn to swim.

When Cash choked, the kid grew still as if he sensed something was terribly wrong. Then he yelled, "Watch me!" He dove, feet splayed too widely apart, sloppily, slamming onto his belly with such force that waves splashed out of the pool.

Cash jumped up as the kid went under, sinking deeper and deeper. Just as Cash was about to fling himself into the pool, the kid's black head bobbed to the surface like a cork. The little daredevil shot Cash a quick smile and shook his wet hair out of his eyes.

For someone so little, the kid was one hell of a swimmer. Sophie...

Don't think about her.

There were so many triumphs Cash would never get to share with Sophie. He remembered her wide smile and the way she'd run to the door on her short chubby legs, brown curls flying, every night when he'd come home, and thrown her arms out, signaling she wanted to be picked up. If he hadn't done so, she'd climbed him, searching his pockets for the little presents he often brought her, as he carried her to find Susana.

Something hot and wet splashed Cash's cheek, and he brushed the dampness away as if it were acid.

"Watch me do another one!"

The kid grinned at him so trustingly that Cash's heart ached. Sophie's grin had been like that.

It had been a mistake to sit down, to watch Miguelito. Cash had broken his rule and let his guard slip. The mortal wound was too raw still. He swallowed, and his throat seemed to tighten. He brought a fist to his lips. When would the grief ever quit eating him alive?

Why didn't I know how much I loved them before it was too late? If only I'd been home....

"Gotta go, kid. I'm late."

Miguelito's smile faded.

Cash bolted to his feet. Spot stood up too, tail wagging so hard it thumped Cash's leg.

"What about the bees?"

"Your aunt— I'm supposed to eat—"

"What's wrong?"

"Nothing!"

Cash loped toward the opposite side of the lawn with Spot hot on his heels. He was glad to get away, until he saw Isabela sexily posed on a yellow-and-white chaise longue beneath thick dripping curtains of orange bougainvillea. She lifted a glass of iced tea, saluting before putting her red lips to the glass's rim and sipping.

The urge to run nearly overpowered him even as he reminded himself that she was perfect for him. She was flamboyantly beautiful. She understood his kind of life. Men would envy him as they'd envied him Susana. But what if he never came to love her?

Isabela's tight red shorts and low-cut white T-shirt clung to her voluptuous curves. When she licked a droplet of condensation off the side of her glass and smiled at him again, guilt made the little hammers in his head pound even harder.

Damn—why wasn't his blood zinging the way it had when he'd been awakened by shy, gorgeous Aphrodite?

If only he'd proposed last night, maybe Isabela and he would have had this damn mating ritual behind them and they could relax and enjoy each other at her beach house today.

Blast Spot for going berserk under Vivian's infernal balcony last night. When Cash had followed the damn dog, he'd sensed something or somebody up there. Then Isabela had told him the balcony was Vivian's. Isabela had gone on to tell him more than he'd needed to know about her sister-in-law.

As he'd listened, he'd felt sympathy toward this woman he hadn't even met. Ever since Vivian had appeared stark naked first thing this morning, his thoughts about her had gotten a powerful grip on his imagination. Just the thought of her was enough to make his body throb.

Again, as if Isabela sensed something amiss she got up and padded toward him. When he didn't take her into his arms, she twined her arms around his neck and pulled him close.

Strangely, the heat of her half-naked breasts pressed into his chest just made him feel uncomfortably sweaty. Then she kissed him, and her kiss was as practiced and perfect as any man could wish for. Her lips clung, her long fingernails caressed his nape.

He sighed heavily. The urge to escape intensified. Last night when she'd kissed him after they'd danced under Vivian's balcony, he'd felt a little sick. The music had seemed too loud, the wine too strong, his jet lag too wearying. All those damn candles had begun to blur...and her hands, all over him, had made him dizzy.

Funny, he'd liked her enthusiasm in Mexico City.

"You smell good," he whispered, his voice cool as he let his arms fall away. "I'm starved," he said, backing away from her. "I can't wait to see the beach house. Marco designed it too?"

"Yes." With a little frown, she held up her hand and signaled a maid. "I saw you with Miguelito, *mi precioso*—at the pool."

"Your nephew, right?" He sat down, thankful to have a table between them.

"Vivian's little emperor," she said.

"Where is she, by the way, your Vivian?"

"I—I'm afraid she can't make it down to breakfast." Isabela frowned.

Faking indifference, he leaned back in the chair, his long legs sprawling beneath the table. His heart actually ached.

"Don't be hurt." Isabela sat down opposite him. "Vivian can be, well, I hate to say this about someone I love so much...but exasperating and unpredictable."

That was easy to believe.

"She does her own thing, if you know what I mean."

Like popping into my room naked?

"When she isn't teaching, she works in a Mayan village, helping the women," Isabela continued.

"How?"

"She teaches them crafts—so they can be independent." She sighed. "I think the men in the village wish she'd go away and stay away. She's giving the women ideas."

Cash stared at Vivian's empty chair at the table and felt increasingly gloomy that she was avoiding him. "You said Vivian was from New Orleans."

"She was an archaeology student. Very intense until she fell so madly in love with Julio. You should have seen them. They were on fire for each other."

Cash shook his head, not liking the image her words conveyed. "You said she was very artistic too."

"That's why she went downtown to the market."

"Downtown?"

"She had to help this Mayan artisan arrange his straw products. Like I said, she works in the villages a lot. When I reminded her she'd promised to meet you, she ran out the door."

"She ran?" He hoped Isabela missed the appalling rasp in his voice.

"It isn't you. The divorce changed her. She hasn't liked men much—or the idea of marriage—since Julio. She's even been strange about you. The first time I showed her pictures of you, she said such odd things."

A weird pain mushroomed in Cash's heart. "You said Julio cheated on her?"

"Men will be men. At least in Mexico. She's too sensitive. But then her parents died when she was very young. Afterward she went to live with an uncle nobody approved of and a friend of his, a dancer I believe. From what I gather it was an...unconventional household—perhaps not entirely appropriate for a young girl. Still, she loved her uncle very much, and she took his death hard too.''

Cash's heart softened toward the young orphaned girl.

''Her parents had been very much in love. I'm afraid they left her with a highly romanticized notion of marriage.''

''So, you think it's okay for men to cheat?''

''No. Not usually. But Vivian never wore makeup or pretty clothes. Then she got so fat and swollen when she was pregnant. She was sick a lot too.''

Cash imagined a young girl in a strange land who'd been misunderstood, pregnant, sick, her emotions in turmoil. It sounded like she'd had no one, not even her husband, to turn to.

''Clearly Vivian won you over at some point.''

''As soon as Miguelito was born, I began to adore her.'' Isabela explained, ''She's a wonderful, selfless mother. He was a sickly baby at first.''

''My wife had a difficult pregnancy,'' Cash said. ''I didn't cheat on her.''

''Well, Julio said she gave Miguelito more attention than she gave him. But I don't want to talk about her.'' Isabela's hand curled over his.

Cash's fingers remained stiff. He couldn't stop thinking that Vivian deserved a better life. He wanted to go to her, to find her, to apologize for this morning—not to sit here where he had to force every smile.

He was in a strange mood. If the maid hadn't been heading toward them with a breakfast tray and his *huevos motuleros,* he would have made some excuse to Isabela and gone to look for Vivian.

''How's your father feeling?'' he asked after the maid left them alone to enjoy glasses of fresh orange juice, plates of fruit, and *huevos motuleros.*

Warily he observed the dish of *mole,* a favorite, spicy, chocolate-flavored sauce. Marco had splashed it on everything. Cash detested *mole.* Luckily Isabela had served it on the side.

"Papacito?"

Isabela watched him attack his *huevos motuleros,* a dish composed of refried beans, fried eggs, chopped ham and cheese on a tortilla slathered in tomato sauce, bits of fried banana, and peas.

"Better?" she asked. Isabela was watching him as she picked at her fruit.

He kept their conversation to the old days, to impersonal, shared interests. They talked of their impending trip to her beach house this afternoon and her ideas for its renovations.

"I want something much grander," she said.

"Then you shall have it."

He relaxed when she didn't flirt with him, and he could think about the house instead of her. But the more questions he asked about the beach house, the more tense she became.

"What's the matter?" she finally whispered, leaning forward.

"Nothing." He dropped his fork on the stones of the patio and had to shove his chair back to pick it up.

"You're different than you were in the city."

When their eyes met, he looked away. "I'm just tired…jet lag. Maybe I drank too much last night."

He resumed eating, but his eggs were cold and tasteless now, and the pineapple was too sweet. He set his fork down and looked up at her beautiful face. When she smiled, he told himself there was nothing for it but to propose. And yet…

"Isabela, there's something I've got to do before…"

He pushed back his chair and stood up. Then he leaned across the table and took her hand and brought it to his lips. "Wait for me? I'll just be a minute."

Her face grew radiant. "I'll be right here."

Unfortunately, as soon as he was in the pool house and had the black velvet box clenched in his palm, he made the mistake of looking at the seven gilded mirrors. In an instant he was flooded with memories of silken copper-red hair cascading over slim shoulders, of large blue eyes filled with longing.

He snapped the box closed and tossed it back into his suitcase. Before he could ask Isabela to marry him, he had to find Vivian and make things all right between them. Maybe when they met fully clothed and had a real conversation, she would relax, and he would too. Maybe then he could quit obsessing about her and get on with his life. With Isabela.

Maybe…

But first he had to find Vivian.

Six

Cash's taxi careened through the narrow streets like a fighter jet. For a second or two he was so worried about crashing he forgot his quandary about Vivian.

He didn't need this. Without taking his eyes off the road, Cash tossed his jacket onto the seat. When the driver nearly hit a burro and cursed, Cash forced a tight smile and then tapped the driver on the shoulder.

"Despacio," he said. *"Más despacio."*

The driver ignored his suggestion to slow down. Instead of arguing, Cash rolled his long-sleeved shirt up and stuck his left elbow out the cab's window. Some things were bigger than he was.

Like what you feel about Aphrodite.

Suppressing the ridiculous thought, he grinned again. If these were his last few minutes alive, he might as well try to enjoy them.

Not that he could. He kept remembering Vivian as colonial buildings and the pandemonium of bulldozers and power drills rushed past him in a blur. Normally, he paid attention to old buildings and new construction sites.

Not possible with the cab jouncing over ruts and holes. Not possible when the exhaust fumes were so dense he could barely breathe.

Isabela? Vivian? He felt ensnared between the two. Isabela had clung to him for an eternity before letting him get in this suicidal cab, begging him to take her with him.

Cash had peeled her hands loose from his forearms and tried to calm her, promising he'd be back in an hour.

"What about my beach house?"

"We'll go the second I get back."

"It will be too hot," she'd pouted.

"Patience, my love."

"Am I your love?"

He hadn't answered her.

It was hot and getting hotter fast. His shirt stuck to his body and his thick hair felt damp against his scalp. Still, despite the heat and the stench of the thick fumes of diesel that belched from the exhaust pipe of the truck in front of his cab, he couldn't help noting that Mérida was more appealing than most cities in Mexico. Maybe it was the colonial architecture painted in pale pastel shades that made the city look so clean.

Not that Cash was thinking all that fondly of Mérida. The poverty in Mexico always got to him. The bleak hopelessness he saw in so many people's eyes was the same even in this sparkling city.

When Cash spied the twin spires of the yellow cathedral, he tapped the driver's thick shoulder again and told him he'd walk the rest of the way. No sooner was he on the street then he regretted his decision. If the cab had been hot, the sidewalk was broiling.

He slung his jacket over his wide shoulder. Even so, he soon felt like an egg frying on a preheated griddle.

Motionless *campesinos,* their backs plastered against the windowless facade of the cathedral, drooped low on their haunches, their dark, dead-looking gazes following him. No doubt their bodies were boiled. Cash felt even sorrier for the Indian women seated on the sidewalk near the church's massive Corinthian doors of solid wood and brass nails. They extended their hands toward him even while they suckled their babies. He passed out coins and dollar bills until his pockets were empty.

When he spotted the House of Montejo on the opposite side of the square, he paused. A bank now, the wonderful old colonial building was the oldest in Mérida, having been completed in 1549 by Francisco de Montejo, a city founder.

A glance at his watch and he moved on. The sidewalk became more crowded the nearer he got to the market, which was located behind the Palacio Municipal.

"Permiso," he droned, avoiding the beggars' eyes because he had no more money to hand out.

"Pasale," they replied.

Against his better judgment, he plunged into the bowels of the cavernous market, which was made up of shops covered with makeshift roofs of faded canvas and tin. Inside, the stifling air reeked of fried food, hemp, cayenne, green spices, curry, leather and disinfectant. After the day's blinding brightness, the cramped aisles and crowded stalls seemed dark and confining. He wandered among sandal shops, candy stores, hammock makers and piñatas. Soon the stalls and merchandise made him feel like he was in a maze. Would he even recognize Aphrodite—dressed?

Smiling vendors jumped in front of him. "Sandals. From Campeche. Handmade, *señor.*"

"Señor, guayaberas?" A man flapped a short-sleeved shirt with four pockets and distinctive vertical rows of double stitching at Cash.

Cash shook his head politely. Swiftly he moved past tables of leatherette watchbands, used magazines, videocassettes of pirated American movies, leather backpacks, silver and coral jewelry, as well as embroidered *huipiles.*

"Souvenir? Live pet beetle?" A pretty girl with jet-black hair, pale brown skin and high cheekbones, as well as the Mayan's hooked nose, jumped in front of Cash and pointed to her arms that were crawling with beetles.

"No, *gracias,*" he murmured, holding his hands up.

Suddenly he'd had enough. Vivian would just have to get over her embarrassment and return to Isabela's on her own. He'd never find her in this labyrinth.

Stumbling blindly down the aisles, he banged into hanging piñatas and got hopelessly tangled in a *rebozo*. Luckily a Mayan girl gave him directions.

He was striding toward a street entrance when a redheaded woman in a shapeless, brightly embroidered white *huipil* and a black skirt looked up and saw him. Screaming, she dived under a table, knocking sandals and hats everywhere.

He knew *that* scream and *that* shade of copper-red hair.

"Vivian!" he shouted.

When he lunged for her, she kicked a stool at him. He tripped over it and went sprawling on the concrete. He was scrambling to his feet when he caught a glimpse of her copper curls under the counter.

"Aphrodite?"

A young man with a thin black mustache offered him a hand up.

His eyes narrowing on the woman, Cash shook his head and flattened himself on the concrete. "Vivian?"

"Go away!"

"Come out from behind there."

She made an animal sound that hung low in her throat and crouched lower, trying to conceal her bright head behind a counter leg.

"I've been looking for you everywhere," he said as she began to crawl backward. When she didn't respond, he added, "There's a wall behind you—filled with hats. The jig's up."

They stood up slowly, not taking their eyes off each other. She was wearing Mexican silver jewelry with amethysts, the white *huipil,* the local blouse lots of the Mayan women wore, a black skirt, and huaraches.

"You've gone native," he muttered.

"Why aren't you at the beach with Isabela?" she whispered. "Why aren't you ever where you're supposed to be?"

"Do you know heem, Mees?" The young man with the mustache was picking up his sandals and hats and frowning at Cash.

"We're friends," Cash said, dusting himself off. "Give us some privacy, *amigo.*"

"I don't know him, Huicho," Vivian said. "Sell the gringo a hat or some sandals for his big feet."

Huicho grabbed Cash with one arm and pulled a wide-brimmed straw hat off a shelf. But when she tried to bolt, Cash lunged and seized her by the wrist. She wriggled, but he yanked her closer.

"Forget it, kid. I have a big head."

Smiling, Huicho patted his hat. *"Muy grande, señor."*

"Let me go!" she snapped, squirming.

"When you calm down, maybe I will."

She quit struggling and stared at him until he released her.

"Why aren't you with Isabela?" she asked, as Cash took the hat Huicho kept shoving toward his head.

"I don't know," he said, plopping the hat on his head with a scowl. "Why would I prefer your company to hers?"

He pulled the absurd hat off and handed it back to the mustached man. "See—head too big. Feet too big for your sandals, too."

"You're supposed to take Isabela to the beach house," Vivian insisted.

"You and I need to talk first."

Huicho held up another hat and Cash grimaced so fiercely, the young man skidded backward several steps.

"Did you ever hear the term 'Ugly American'?" she whispered.

"In that sissy hat I'd damn sure fit the bill."

She laughed, and the sound lit him up. Then she shyly hid her beautiful mouth behind her slender fingers so he couldn't see she was smiling. "The hat messed up your leonine mane."

"My leonine what?"

"Your beautiful hair," she said softly, reaching up and smoothing it.

She likes my hair.

"There. That's better," she said as she tucked a damp raven lock behind his ear.

He had a thing about his hair, and the instant she stroked it, he went rigidly still, his breath indrawn. Her fingertip against his ear had his blood zinging. His mood changed instantly.

Then her hand fell away, but the zing got worse. She couldn't seem to move either, and her hand hovered near his face, tempting him to touch her too.

"Feels better," he whispered, his voice tight.

Slowly, but still staring at him in that funny, dazed way he found so appealing, she lowered her hand a little, her curled fingers helplessly digging into her palm.

"This is bad," she whispered. "I shouldn't— *We* shouldn't—"

"Yes." They were in this god-awful market. People like Huicho were watching. But Cash's blood was on fire. He liked her body, her face, her eyes. He liked talking to her, being with her. Most of all, he liked the heat in her blue gaze when she looked at him.

It felt like fate, and he didn't believe in fate. But how could you not believe in something that was happening to you?

"This is very bad," he repeated, even as he felt a powerful desire to taste her.

"I never meant—"

His hand closed over her wrist, and it was his turn to stroke her in reverent wonder. What was it about her? There'd been the occasional pretty woman that had made him zing. But he'd been busy. He'd had a life. Nobody had ever gotten to him like she did. Not this fast. Not this powerfully. And he didn't trust it.

"I mean I shouldn't have touched—" She broke off.

He knew what she meant, and he knew better than to touch her, too. Still, he continued to stroke her arm, lightly, ever so lightly because he couldn't seem to stop. Her skin was soft and warm, just liked he'd known she'd be.

"I'm glad you did," he said. "Why did you stop?" He put her hand against his temple, and the heat of her splayed fingertips against his scalp made him feel like he was drowning in pleasure. She was becoming addictive. For a moment he couldn't breathe.

One minute parakeets were chirping, piñata vendors were yelling, and a little girl was weeping for fried candy. A bunch of rowdy kids in big jeans and T-shirts raced by carrying boom boxes.

Then Vivian's fingertips slid against his temple, and the sounds in the market died to nothing. The boom boxes shut down like clams. Traffic noises—honking, brakes squealing— all gone.

He couldn't hear a damn thing. Everything else seemed to slow down too. Mainly he noticed his sluggish, heavy breathing as well as the violent thudding of his heart.

Her lips moved, but no sound came out. Or maybe it did and he just couldn't hear. She had a beautiful mouth, and all of a sudden, more than anything, he wanted his lips on hers. He had to taste their sweet, voluptuous heat.

"You're going to marry Isabela," she said helplessly.

"That was the plan," he admitted, but the plan seemed alien and all wrong to him now.

"I think you got the incorrect impression. This morning...when you saw me..."

"Naked?" he supplied helpfully, smiling.

The word and smile set off sparks. Her eyes flashed and her cheeks flamed, and he got hot all over too.

She lowered her voice. "I was embarrassed."

"Ditto."

"It's not ditto. You got naked deliberately."

"To make you feel more at ease."

"You make it sound like it was a gentlemanly act."

"It was." The need to taste her soft lips was intense.

"Well, it didn't work, and that's not why you did it."

"I know why I do the stuff I do."

"Well, then admit men enjoy getting women in compromising situations. They like to create a sexual environment...so *anything* might happen."

Like a kiss.

"I know how men like you think," she continued.

"You just think you do."

"Isabela thinks you're special. But you've got a dirty mind."

"You tempted me."

She turned red again. "If you're so pure—why aren't you with her?"

He wanted to kiss her. He wanted to take her in his arms and put his hands all over her, to push his aroused body against hers, to see how they fit together. Hell, maybe she did have him pegged.

What he wanted was to slam her against the shelves of sombreros and bang her and get this crazy thing between them over with—once and for all.

He wanted to hold her tenderly too.

Which was exactly why he wasn't about to touch her—not with a ten-foot pole. Besides, he was hot, burning up in fact. And not because the market was a noxious-smelling oven.

"You want to know if I'd be an easy conquest," she said. "Because I'm a divorcée."

"I don't give a damn about you being a divorcée," he muttered, stepping toward her. "But the other part—the easy conquest part... Well, are you?"

"See! I'm right about you." She backed up fast.

"I was just teasing," he retorted grumpily.

"Well, don't tease. I'm not in the mood. You're too big and this space is too tight. Besides, it's too damn hot."

And you're too damn sexy. He wiped his brow.

Huicho was holding a stack of hats, waiting politely to get Cash's attention, his black eyes glued on them.

"Can we go somewhere else?" Cash murmured, ignoring the vendor. "I could buy you a coffee."

"No. I'm too hot for coffee."

"You should've said yes to coffee," Cash murmured. "Then I wouldn't have to do this—"

"What?"

"Convince you to have a talk before this thing—whatever it is—gets out of hand."

"If you'd just leave, nothing would get out of hand. Isabela is waiting. And none too patiently—I promise you."

Isabela? Suddenly he didn't give a damn about Isabela. Not when Vivian's eyes and body and mouth lured him like magnets.

"This is your fault, you know," he said.

"Men always blame sex on the woman."

"Sex? Don't ever forget you suggested it."

"Not here," she shrieked, genuinely alarmed.

He smiled. Telling himself to move slowly, he took another step toward her. As if he were a snake about to strike, Vivian sprang backward, straight into the shelves piled high with hats.

"Mis sombreros," Huicho cried as his shelves tilted, causing dozens of hats and lots of sandals to rain down on them.

Cash had never forced a woman before, and he never would—especially not in a public place. Then she screamed again, and vendors popped out of the woodwork to gape. To shut her up, Cash seized Vivian by the arms and crushed his mouth down on hers, hard.

At first her body was rigid and her lips stiff and unyielding.

"Let me go!" She pounded at his chest with puny fists.

"Hush!" His grip tightened. After that he was lost.

Next thing he knew, his tongue was in her mouth and he had her pinned to the wall. Her wriggling body against his felt better than anything he'd ever imagined, and hotter too. Perspiration dripped from her hair onto his hands. Desire spiraled through him.

Feeling as if his world had gone insane and he'd gone even crazier, he released her mouth and muttered, both savagely and tenderly, "I've never done this before. I swear to you."

"I hate you," she spat. "I'll hate you forever if you don't stop—"

"Just with you," he growled. "This has only happened with you. Usually I'm the sanest man alive. Boringly sane."

When their mouths came together again, it was like a match falling on gasoline. He exploded, and after that, he couldn't stop kissing her.

As for Vivian, she'd been dazed and furious when she'd left the house. Thinking herself safe from him in the market, she'd been terrified when he'd suddenly appeared, striding straight at her like a tall gringo god.

Then he'd seen her, and after that he hadn't stopped staring at her with those wild green eyes that lured her. *Dios,* how he'd flushed every time he looked at her. *Dios,* how could just his eyes on her mouth turn her to mush?

Now that he was kissing her, with heated, demanding lips, she knew that he was temptation—at least for her—in its purest, rawest form. He was taller, bigger, darker than she remembered. Or at least he seemed so in the shadowy stall. She was like a moth who'd been exiled to the dark and cold too long, a moth who'd beat her wings to death just to be near the flame, even if the wicked tongue of desire burned so hotly she caught fire and was incinerated.

If Cash was here, he was only responding to her signals. This was all her fault. After years of rigid control, her body was betraying her, as she'd always feared it would.

When he grabbed her again, to her horror and embarrassment and immense delight, her hands slid up around his neck and she threw her body into his. Their clothes were damp with perspiration, their skin hotter. She heard him gasp. The fact that he wanted her thrilled her. Her lips opened, and she was kissing him back with an urgency that more than matched his.

Her tongue was in his mouth, and she wanted it there. Heat lit every cell in her body and made her feel achingly alive. Every minute since she'd run out of the pool house, she'd been thinking about how gorgeous he was, every long inch of him. Over and over again she'd relived him ripping off that sheet so she could see him.

Her hands slid around his back, which was warm and muscular and damp. *Dios,* he felt even better than he looked. She wanted to tear his wet shirt off and lick his body as she had in her dream.

Mindlessly, she was running her fingers up the contours of his broad shoulders and raking her fingertips through his silky black hair, thrilled that he groaned and gasped at her slightest touch. He made her feel precious and desirable and all woman.

He was hard and hot and it didn't take a rocket scientist to figure out where this was going. She had to open her eyes, and when she did, she saw half a dozen familiar brown faces from the village. When she blinked, they began to giggle and hide their smirks.

She shut her eyes in mortification. The villagers would never take her seriously again. But the minute her eyes were closed, she became a wanton creature of sensation again, a woman who needed a man to hold her as Cash was holding her. She was blissfully aware only of his mouth and hands, aware only of his taste and her own wildly pulsating hunger for more.

Isabela. He belongs to Isabela.

Vivian had to remember that. But it wasn't easy, not when some deep part of her wanted him so much. The thought that he could never be hers only made her kiss him more desperately and cling more tightly.

When he cupped his hands around her breasts and raked his fingernails across her erect nipples, she pulled him behind a stack of hats on the countertop and pressed her fingers against his fly and touched him through his jeans just to make sure he was as turned on as she was.

He was.

Curls of flaming heat exploded in her blood. She wanted more breathless kisses, more…more… She squeezed him gently through the denim.

He groaned and gripped her tighter. ''Aphrodite, unless you want it here and now in this melting hell hole, on this concrete floor on top of a bunch of straw hats in front of your friends, we'd better clear out of here fast.''

As suddenly as he'd seized her, his big brown hands fell to his sides, where they hung like claws knotted. She could see his pulse hammering in his throat—as hers was. He panted for every breath as she did.

Dios, he wanted her, every bit as much as she wanted him. She imagined a roller-coaster car flying off its track, out of control.

Not good.

''I shouldn't have kissed you.'' His voice was rough and strange even as his eyes drank in her face. His expression hardened.

''If ever there was an understatement…'' She shut her eyes because just looking at his exquisite, carved face with all that wavy black hair falling across his dark brow made her want to forget Isabela and all her sister-in-law meant to her and throw herself into his arms and kiss and touch him all over again.

She wanted to smooth his hair back, to lock her legs around his waist and rub herself against that bulge in his pants. She wanted him inside her. She wanted to climax again and again and then lie in bed with him afterward for hours. *She was insane.*

"I don't know what got into me," he said, forcing out the words between harsh breaths. "I've been like a dead man so long. You're better than a roller-coaster ride."

You too.

"A thrill a minute," she agreed, almost hating herself because it was true.

"So, you're conceited about your immense sex appeal?" His voice was harsh.

"Not really. My car has a tendency to fly off the track—and you know what happens to cars that fly?"

He met her eyes with frank curiosity.

"Gravity," she whispered. "It's always fatal."

"Every time I look at you, I want to devour you," he said, and she heard the hunger in his low, angry tone. "Since the moment I saw you. Before that, even. Since the moment I *felt* you."

"Felt me?"

"When I stood under your balcony last night."

"I was up there…hiding."

"Just looking at you now makes me feel like I'm melting. What the hell's wrong with me? Nothing like this has ever happened to me before— Hell, I'm even repeating myself."

"Well, it's happened to me. Trust me, this is the best part of the ride—the first kiss. The thrill lasts for a while. Then the car flies into the ground and smashes you all to bits. It's not pretty. The aftermath lasts a lot longer than the thrills."

"That's what happened to you and Julio?"

"To me, anyway. Julio just hopped in a brand-new car. I'm not like that—but being a man, you probably are. History has a way of repeating itself. I'm no good at picking men."

"I'm not Julio."

"Lucky you. Lucky Julio. He walked away without a scratch. But not me. And you know what I think? I think you're way more dangerous than Julio. Way, way worse—at least for me. And me is who I have to protect.''

''What?'' The hurt tone in his deep voice as well as the anguish in his dark eyes crushed her.

''You belong to Isabela.''

''Do I? Maybe you don't know everything. Maybe you just think you do.''

''I know all I need to know. So, here's what we're going to do,'' she began.

''How come you get to call the shots? This has thrown me for a loop too.''

''Because I'm experienced at this lust at first sight or love at first sight, and you're not!'' She squared her shoulders. ''I for one want to be more than a sex object. I want to be a real person to the next man I get involved with. So, you're going back to Isabela. You two belong together. Like should marry like.''

''Like should marry like?''

''Yes. So, you're going to the beach house just as you planned. Then I'm taking Miguelito to the park the way we always do. From now on, you and I—we don't see each other or talk to each other until you're gone.''

''All right, on one condition. First, you have coffee with me in one of those *puestos* on the square. We'll talk this out like normal human beings,'' he said. ''We'll make our plan. Then—and only then—I'll agree to avoid you.''

''No—''

''If you don't agree, I'll hop in your car and kiss you again and make your car fly off the track.'' The corner of his mouth lifted.

''I don't care. My life's already smashed to pieces. I've got nothing to lose. A kiss, I can handle.''

''Can you?'' he whispered.

''Watch!'' She moved toward him. When she puckered her lips, he jumped back. ''See, maybe you can't either.''

''You're dangerous,'' he muttered.

"So are you. But not to me. I'm a big girl now. I know better than to go for roller-coaster rides." She tossed her head back, put her hands on her hips and tried to look like she had confidence in what she was saying.

"Coffee, tea—or me?" he murmured in her ear, his breath so warm that she tingled all over.

"That's an old line." She jumped away.

"Whatever works."

She laughed and then pointed to Huicho, who was holding five smashed hats. "I think your size-fifteen shoes flattened a lot of hats."

"Size twelve," he muttered rather defensively, studying his feet.

"Buy them…and I'll have that drink of coffee on the square with you."

"You're easy."

She blushed. "Which is why we're in this mess. But, if I'm easy, you—Mr. Big Shot Big-Footed Famous Architect— you aren't exactly playing hard-to-get yourself."

To her astonishment, he flushed as deeply as she would have had he said that to her. And he was cute—too cute— when he blushed.

"Loan me a couple of twenties," he said.

"What?"

"I'm afraid I gave all my money to the beggars…." He broke off sheepishly.

This was bad. Really bad.

Rich guys weren't supposed to have big hearts.

Seven

"We'd like a table away from the crowd," Cash told the white-coated waiter, who rushed to greet them with a big smile and menus at the entrance of the sidewalk café.

"No."

The last thing Vivian wanted was to be alone with him, but before she could protest, a loud wolf whistle behind her made her turn beet red and whirl around furiously.

A parrot in a giant cage flapped his wings flirtatiously at her as every male customer turned to stare and smirk.

"Somebody besides me thinks you're a very sexy lady," Cash murmured. "I've got a birdbrained rival." Then he saw the other men and returned their glances coldly. "Too many rivals."

"This is Mexico." She laughed nervously and leaned toward the bird's cage. The parrot had forgotten her and was pecking at a pinto bean.

"Pretty boy, you've clearly been around too many macho males."

The bird dropped his bean. "Sexy lady. Sexy lady," he repeated.

"Demanding creature," Cash said as they sat down at a small corner table under a massive stone archway.

"He was cute."

"I bet you wouldn't say that if I whistled like that."

"You did far worse." She blushed.

"All right, may I apologize, then? Will you ever forgive me?"

She froze. "I think it's safer if I stay mad."

"It's not like I committed murder. All I did was kiss you." He shot her a look that made her shiver.

She squeezed her hands together and put them in her lap. "I guess I can try."

"That's very generous of you. Thanks."

She picked up her purse and pulled her cell phone out.

"Expecting a call?"

She turned it off. "No. Avoiding one."

"Julio?"

She nodded. Then she tried to sit straight and stiff and keep her hands in her lap, but Cash was so big and so close that she squirmed and scooted back in her seat in an effort to put some distance between them. But when she did, her bare legs brushed Cash's denim jeans underneath the table. He re-adjusted his long legs to avoid hers, and they banged legs again.

"Sorry—long legs," he said.

She laughed awkwardly and wished she were anywhere in the whole world but here with him.

She stared up at the ceiling fan that whisked warm air overhead. Then she looked down and became fascinated by the way the air stirred Cash's longish black hair that fell against his collar. *That* hair. *Those* eyes. *That* big male body.

Listen to the music—do anything but think about him!

The background music swung from *Madame Butterfly* to heavy metal. The caged parrot squawked at every new customer.

"No other lady's rated a wolf whistle except you, sexy lady," Cash said. "I've been watching the entrance."

She neither looked at him nor commented.

The waiter came, and they ordered. When he brought some of their food, Vivian felt better because she could munch on a little log of her favorite *leche quemada,* a sinful, unique recipe found only in this restaurant consisting of caramelized milk, ground almonds, cinnamon, and sherry. Cash guzzled his coffee. At least she had something to do with her hands and mouth, and the candy was so delicious, maybe it would distract her from how appealing he was. But still, his dark good looks struck her. Even though he was behaving like a gentleman, his warmth and charm made her sizzle.

They sat in silence for a while, and just when she was beginning to think she might survive their attempt to act like two normal human beings around each other, he leaned across the table and tipped his new Panama hat toward her at a rakish angle.

"Does this hat make me look young and sexy?" he said, his green eyes dancing in a way that made her heart do an absurd flip.

"You ask a lot of a hat," she retorted, licking at her candy with the tip of her tongue.

When he watched her tongue flick, she grew self-conscious and tossed her candy on the plate. "What did you want to tell me?"

"Better off or on? What do you think?"

"P-l-e-e-ase," she drawled, staring up at the ceiling fan. "We had a reason for coming here."

Then he took it off and fanned her with it while he made a funny face. She couldn't help giggling. He put it back on and tilted it to one side, so that it cast half his carved face in shadow.

He had broad hands, long fingers, nails that were trimmed just so. Nice hands… *They'd felt good too, burningly, deliciously, sinfully good.*

"On or off?" he persisted.

"Off."

He grimaced and took it off, then combed his hands through his hair. She knew he was trying to make her relax.

"And I had such high expectations." He stared at the hat rather wistfully and then lifted his gorgeous eyes to hers again and begged her to treat him like a normal human being.

Those eyes of his. They shredded her heart.

"High expectations will break your heart," she whispered as she ripped the hat he'd bought for her off her head and placed it on top of his.

"Only if they're wrong." He lifted his black brows and watched as she shook out her hair. "What if they're right?"

"You're probably a better gambler than I."

"There was a crowd in Florence night before last that has me wondering. I built a building that they don't like."

"Is it off with your head, then?" She laughed and sliced a finger across her throat.

He didn't laugh. "They wanted to cut off other parts of my anatomy."

"Let me guess." Her eyes drifted down his broad chest, causing him to flush and shift in his chair. "The family jewels?"

His neck turned purple.

"Do you regret building it?"

"Yes and no. I had to push myself. If you don't push yourself, you go nowhere." His face darkened. "Isn't that what you've been doing down here for the past seven years?"

Hastily she bit off more caramelized candy. "Let's talk about something more interesting than my slow-paced life here."

"Sex?" He grinned.

"Not sex."

"And not your life? I'm all out of subjects."

She drew in a slow breath. "An architect should have a more active imagination."

"You've had my imagination working overtime lately," he murmured, his eyes on her mouth.

The waiter brought the rest of her order—figs and strawberries. She ate a fig while he watched her teeth tear at the fruit. Something in his intense expression made her feel funny in her stomach.

To break the tension, she said, "Thank you for buying the hats. Maybe you ruined my reputation with the villagers forever, but you certainly made Huicho's day."

"No more Ugly American?"

The waiter walked by holding the parrot on a gloved hand. The parrot bellowed, "Ugly American," and people turned to stare.

"I don't much like parrots," Cash said.

"Ugly American," the bird screamed again, and the waiter carried him away.

"The term definitely doesn't apply to you." Her gaze drifted over him assessingly, lingering on his eyes and long, curling lashes and then on his thick, black hair.

"So, you think I'm handsome?"

"Maybe just a little." She felt her cheeks heat at the admission.

"If you thought I was any more handsome, we'd be back in the market naked, doing it on those damn hats. I'd have had to buy out the entire village."

"Wrong subject, remember?" She twisted a red curl around her fingertip so tightly the end of her finger went numb.

"Right. Your Huicho was beaming like a happy fox after you helped him rip me off."

"You're rich. He's poor."

"The perpetual class war. We rich are constantly under attack—"

"You wanted to talk…so talk. I need to get back to Miguelito. And away from you," she finished in a softer tone.

"Okay, let's not let a perfectly innocent accident and impulsive reaction, er, action on my part...in the market...ruin our relationship.''

''Relationship? We don't have a relationship.''

''We got naked together and we kissed.''

''Which is why I told you we have to avoid each other— not sit here together and discuss it. You're supposed to have a relationship with Isabela.''

''That was the plan.'' His expression darkened.

''She's rich and unencumbered by a child. Her father's a famous architect—your mentor. You know the same people. She's been wonderful to me.''

''You don't have to sell Isabela to me. Marrying her was my bright idea, remember.''

''What you and I have to do is avoid one another.''

''So, you think I should go back to Plan A?''

''Plan A being Isabela?'' she asked.

He nodded.

''Of course. We already agreed on that. We'll chalk this...us...up to temporary insanity. Seeing someone naked would make anybody crazy—especially a man.''

''You didn't feel a thing?''

His smile made her shiver deep inside her belly. ''I say we stay away from each other. I'll let Isabela introduce us formally, of course. Maybe over lunch. Then I disappear with Miguelito. In other words, we avoid each other like the plague.''

''And in a day or two, I should have my car back on the right track, so to speak?''

''Exactly. You weren't really flying. You were just up in the air an inch or two.''

He laughed. ''It damn sure felt like flying.''

''Don't think about it, then. You'll get well faster.''

''Right. So, what's it like...being down here with a kid?''

She dropped her gaze to the platter of figs. ''I think you and I have everything figured out. I need to go.''

He was watching her so intently her breath caught. He had

a way of seeing too much, and she wondered what she was doing here with him. Feeling more and more at ease with him. When Isabela, beloved Isabela, was at home.

No way could she relate to him. He had years and years of schooling. He was great at what he did—famous too. He knew who he was, and she still didn't have a clue who she was.

She'd dropped out after one year of college. He probably thought she was so far beneath him, they weren't even on the same planet.

She swallowed again. "So, what's it like being rich and famous?"

"If we're going to talk, I asked you first. What's it like for you—here?"

"As if you care."

"You could open up. Sometimes it's easier to talk to strangers. What do you want? What do you dream about?"

You. Love. Happily ever after.

She shook her head. "I was a young, stupid fool. I wanted the perfect love. So, I married a man I didn't know. I was idealistic. I thought he was someone he could never be. He's not a bad man. He's…he's…just not husband material. Not for me anyway."

"And what kind of man would be husband material?"

"Who would want me? What do I have to offer the kind of man I'd want to marry? I've got a kid, no education and no future. I think I need to fix me first."

"If you think you need to have something to offer, why aren't you busy acquiring the skills and talents you need to get what you want? Go get an education."

"Like it's that easy? I have a kid."

"So? He's cute and friendly. He could be an asset."

"I'm flat broke."

"Do you intend to stay that way the rest of your life? If you don't, when are you going to start doing something about it?" he persisted.

"I let Julio steal my inheritance."

"The trouble with you is you're stuck in the past."

"This conversation is getting way too personal. Besides, you're making me mad."

"What are you, twenty-six? Maybe it's time you grew up and did something to solve your problems."

"Twenty-five," she snapped. "And you know what? You're clueless. You don't know me. You don't know anything. You can't tell me how to solve my problems. Not when you were born with a silver spoon in your mouth."

"Then whine and dream till you die for all I care."

"Shut up. Just shut up."

"Sorry." He slid back in his chair. "I was out of line. Way out of line. What I meant was, you should quit feeling sorry for yourself and set some goals. You know a lot of women would just wait for some white knight to show up and rescue them."

"Not me. Never again."

"You could try playing the sex object. You're pretty good at it." He lifted a dark brow.

"No man's going to rescue me. There's no such thing as a hero. I've learned that much. Men—all men, including you cause way more problems than they ever solve. Sex makes more trouble than it solves, too." She got up. "This conversation is getting us nowhere. Thanks for breakfast. I learned a lot. You and I were better off before we talked. Isabela is my sister-in-law. And she's very jealous. Mérida is a small town. If someone sees us here—"

"She trusts you completely."

"And I want to keep it that way."

"Not so fast. You told me your life story, and I gave you free advice."

"Which is all it's worth."

"Well, now it's my turn."

"What?"

"You owe me." He grabbed one of her figs and began munching, rather loudly.

"You can be obnoxious sometimes." She seized a fig too and against her will sat back down and began to toy with it. But he was fun to kiss, and even when he exasperated her, he had fierce male energy that made her feel cared for.

He laughed. "Maybe I'll tell you what it's like being rich. It's not what you think. It sets you apart, makes you cold, inhuman. My father was the coldest man I ever knew. I didn't really love Susana when I married her the way you loved Julio, and I didn't think there was anything wrong with that. She was beautiful and smart and well-educated and well-bred, the sort of woman a man in my position was expected to marry."

"Like Isabela?"

"Not exactly." Still, he nodded and shot her a thin smile. "I enjoyed her company, and the longer I was with her, the closer I felt to her. But I worked too hard and was gone all the time. Then we had a little girl. In the last year before they were... There was a fire, you see...."

"Isabela told me. I'm so sorry."

He stopped talking abruptly and went still. Then he stared out the window at the street. "Well..." He gulped in a deep breath and then another, as if unable to go on.

Just watching him caused a lump to form in her throat.

"You came to love her. I can tell."

"Yes. I didn't grow up accustomed to love. I'd never known what it was. So love came as a surprise to me."

"My parents died when I was a little girl," she began softly. "Just like that—everything was gone. People vanish, and there's this big hole in your life you can never fill."

He looked up at her. "And you don't know what they meant to you until they're gone. It was as if there were all these barrels of love inside me. While she was alive they'd been shut up tight. When she died, they overflowed, and suddenly I was drowning."

"I thought my little brother was such a pest. Then—" She stopped and shut her eyes. "An uncle I hadn't really known took me in. He showed up right after the funeral. I told him I didn't want to be adopted. And you know what he said?''

"What?'' Cash was staring at her intently.

"'How about you adopt me, then?' There were tears in his gray eyes—eyes that reminded me of my father's, only his face was softer, kinder. He knelt and I hugged him. And after a while my life got all right again, better than all right. In fact my life with Uncle Morton and his friends was wonderful…if unconventional.'' She wasn't quite ready to tell him about Uncle Morton. "It set me apart, but it broke down a lot of barriers. Your money separated you, but I learned people are just people, that labels are just labels. And that they aren't really right most of the time.''

When Cash stared out at the noisy street at a man who was sweeping the trash into piles, she resumed talking even though she wasn't sure he was listening. "I wanted to grow up and fall in love. To have children. To be happy like my parents. I thought it would be so easy to marry and be part of a happy family.''

He selected another fig. "Then you met Julio.''

"And at first it was easy, but it didn't work out.''

He nodded. "Go on.''

"You said I need to grow up. Maybe I have already. I thought I loved Julio so much. That's why I'm afraid of marriage now…afraid of trusting my instincts again. I wouldn't want to give so much of myself just to lose it all again. Miguelito loves so easily. I don't want his heart broken. I want life to be different, but I'm afraid of repeating my mistakes.''

"Maybe you have to try anyway.'' He stared at her. "All I wanted when I came here was to marry again, I guess because I couldn't bear living alone.''

"You make living with someone sound so easy…as if anyone will do.''

"Maybe I was being stupid,'' he said thoughtfully.

"I'm not sure you can just pick whomever you want. People can't be replaced,'' she said.

"I know. But I guess it's all in those expectations we talked about. Maybe I wasn't expecting nearly as much as you. Maybe I thought anybody would be better than the emptiness I felt."

"Isabela deserves to be loved too."

"I believed I would fall in love as I did with Susana." His eyes darkened with pain.

"It's not your fault, you know—what happened to your little girl and wife."

"Any more than Julio's cheating and your marriage ending is yours. You were simply incompatible, and now you must plan a new life."

"Plan?" She smiled. "You make it sound easy. You've built a big life while I have a small one that is nothing like I envisioned. Lots of mornings I wake up and wonder, what am I doing here?"

"Miguelito adores you."

"Yes—he does."

"So, quit listening to your demons. Your life isn't so small. It has meaning, and my big life feels pretty empty. Follow your dreams, and you'll be fine."

Her eyes shone, and then she remembered about Sophie and all he'd lost, and she couldn't look at him. "I'm sorry," she whispered, putting her hand over his.

He flinched as if her fingers stung his warm, solid hand. Then he went rigid, and she knew it was because she'd touched him. Suddenly she remembered their kiss, and maybe he did too. The air became suffocating, and when his eyes met hers, she was intensely aware of him.

He looked at their locked hands and up at her, and his eyes took her breath away. There was so much she wanted to tell him, but she couldn't seem to frame a single coherent thought. So their gazes did the talking.

Mammal to mammal, man to woman, they were right together in ways that had nothing to do with intellectual thought or words or even sex. He sighed as if he found much comfort in her touch and in her friendship, and then, to her surprise, he put his other hand on hers, keeping it there until the waiter came with the bill.

"Friends?" Cash whispered at last, lifting a brow as he reached for his wallet and pulled out a credit card to pay.

"Friends...but *just* friends," she emphasized. "We shouldn't have talked," she whispered.

"'We shouldn't.'" He grinned teasingly. "Why do you keep saying that?"

She pulled her cell phone out of her purse along with a card with a taxi's number on it and placed a brief call.

When they walked out of the restaurant together into the brilliant sunshine that hit her like a blast furnace, the parrot squawked. "Taxi! Taxi!"

"Wonderful bird...mind reader," she said, shading her eyes with her hand when she looked up at Cash.

"And I thought we'd come to an understanding about that awful bird."

She laughed. "He's a fan of mine."

"So am I."

For a brief shining moment she felt he knew her better than anyone she'd ever met. Which was crazy.

Then he took her hand and brought it up to his lips slowly, as if he could not resist. His lips were gentle, but they burned, sending a message straight to her heart.

"See you later," she said too quickly.

He gave her a slow smile that melted every bone in her body as he let her go.

A cab rushed up to them spewing dark fumes, and Cash opened her door.

She smiled. "I called him for you. I have my own car. Two blocks away."

"It's too hot to walk. I'll drop you."

When she bent from the waist to get into the back seat, she heard a wolf whistle that made her jump and whirl angrily around, until she saw it was just the parrot, up to his old tricks.

Cash said, "At least that troublemaking bird and I agree about something. You've got the cutest butt in Mérida."

"I think I'll walk—"

"The hell you will!" He pushed her unceremoniously into the back seat, threw himself inside and slammed the door.

"You're evil," she said, leaning forward to give the cabbie directions.

"Sorry I made that comment about your…er…backside. Blame it on Mexico," Cash murmured. "It does something to a man."

Before Vivian could think up an adequate retort, her cell phone rang. When she pulled it out of her purse, Isabela's shrill, terrified voice nearly burst her eardrum.

"Come home—now!"

"I'm on my way, *querida.*"

"Quickly, just come quickly. Something terrible has happened!"

Eight

Vivian sensed chaos even before she got out of her car.

Eusebio held on to Miguelito's hand and Concho's new collar until Vivian could properly park in the carport and turn off the engine, but the minute he let go, Miguelito and Concho sprang toward her.

"Tía Isabela's been stung by bees! African bees! Hundreds and hundreds of them!" Miguelito, his eyes huge, clapped his cheeks and moaned. "They tried to get me when I was swimming too! They were in the wall behind the purple flowers with the stickers."

"Bougainvillea. Thorns," she said. "But why?"

"When Pedro was using the weed eater, they really started buzzing." He made sweeping motions with his arms. "They were a big black cloud. One landed on Tía's arm and she swatted it. Then they all got mad at her and chased her!"

"Where is she?"

Miguelito grabbed his mother's hand and buried his head in her skirt. He held her fingers tightly, and she ran her hand through his black hair. "In her bed. Will she die?" he whispered.

"Of course not, darling."

"Pedro called the doctor," Eusebio said. "Señorita Isabela, she is crying like a little child."

Vivian cupped Miguelito's chin. "No wonder you're so scared. *Qué barbaridad.*"

Miguelito looked up at her with big liquid-dark eyes. "Tía ran round and round in circles. Then she jumped into the pool and the bees kept buzzing the water. Every time she popped her head out, they stung her again. Then Pedro threw her some towels, and they chased him into the pool house." He gulped in a deep breath. "I was hiding in there, and one stung my nose. See!"

She knelt. He held still, so that she could inspect it properly. There was a microscopic red bump on the tip of his dusky nose.

"Oh, *mi precioso.*" She hugged him close.

"Sí, me duele," he whimpered. *It hurts.* He squinched up his eyes, but he couldn't quite manage a tear.

"We'll get some magic cream to put on it."

"Can I watch cartoons the rest of the day?"

Normally cartoons were forbidden.

"Of course, *mi precioso.*"

"Will Tía really be all right?"

When she nodded, he smiled radiantly.

Grabbing his hand, she raced with him to Isabela's vast bedroom, which was dark and cool after the brilliant, hot sun.

"Isabela?" Vivian opened the door softly.

A dramatic moan followed by a sob came from the bed. A voice that cracked after every syllable wailed, "My face is swo-llen like a watermelon! You can't let *him* see me! Not like this!"

"Isabela—"

When Vivian raced across the room, Isabela smothered her

face in her pillow. Vivian petted her black, silky hair. Slowly, after Isabela calmed a little, she peeled the pillow away.

"I'm so ugly," Isabela sobbed, and then she beat the pillow with her fists.

"At least you're not allergic."

Miguelito climbed onto the bed and stared at his aunt's purple face. Black eyeliner ran down her wet cheeks. His beautiful mouth made an O. Then, with a gasp, he drew back and clung to his mother, hiding his face in her skirts again.

"See—even *mi precioso* is afraid of me!"

"Are you in pain?" Vivian asked.

"The doctor gave me several shots. So, no. But you have to entertain Cash for me…until I'm better."

Vivian shook her head. "I've got way too much to do."

"You have to, Vivi. He can't see me like this. Things haven't been going well between us. I don't know what I'm doing wrong. He's so cold all of a sudden. And now this! Maria says a *bruja* has cast a spell. She saw a dead bird nailed to the door last night. She says that's a sign. She sent for a white witch to counteract it."

Vivian never ceased to be amazed that beneath the thin overlay of Catholic faith and the rational mind-set of its European conquerors, the Mexican people had at their core a passionate belief in native mysticism and ancient magic.

"Forget about witches. Be logical. Cash cares about your inner beauty. He'll sympathize. You can spend the day together here—talking and getting to know one another."

Isabela's swollen face contorted. "Don't you know anything?" She paused. "This is *his* fault. We had a date, plans, and he ran off and left me all alone this morning. He wouldn't tell me where he was going. I—I had a wonderful picnic basket packed—"

"Then you stay here. Eusebio is back. He can drive Cash to the beach house to sketch. I don't—"

"By himself?" Isabela seized her by the wrist. "You have

to go with him, but don't take him to the beach house. Maybe I'll be well tomorrow and able to take him myself.''

''I have plans with Miguelito.''

''Take him with you too. Show Cash some ruins. Uxmal is so lovely…and then go to Loltún.'' Loltún was an underground cave with a beautiful pool.

Vivian gasped, not trusting herself to be alone with Cash. ''You're not listening.''

''You have to do this. Cash is restless. What if he grows bored and goes home? What if he doesn't propose?''

Vivian shook her head.

''He has a ring. A huge beautiful engagement ring just my size. Maria was cleaning his room. She saw it.''

''You got Maria to spy for you?''

''If he doesn't marry me, I won't go to the United States. Then I won't be able to take you with me.''

''I—I'm not sure my going with you is such a good idea anyway—''

''*Querida,* I'm desperate. Pathetic, I know. But I love him. Look at me. I'm so ugly. You have to help me.'' Isabela was trembling.

''I want to help you, but trust me, I just can't do this one thing. I would do anything else. Why can't Julio go?''

''Julio made Tammy jealous and they had a fight. He's sulking and won't answer his phone. I've left four messages. You're the only person I trust with Cash. You can tell him wonderful stories about me. He'll believe you.''

Vivian flushed as she remembered their kiss in the market.

''I love you—like my very own sister,'' Isabela continued. *Which is why I'm the last person who should go.*

''Think of everything I've done for you—and for Miguelito—when you had nobody else to help you. Just me.''

For a heartbeat, Vivian wanted to confess…stripping… kissing…

Isabela's voice dropped to a teary whisper. ''You'll do it, yes?''

Vivian put a fingertip to her lips, and just touching them made her flush at the memory of Cash's mouth on hers.

"I can't! I simply can't!"

"What happened to avoiding each other?" Cash asked, his eyes wickedly alight as he helped Eusebio sling the heavy wicker picnic basket in the back of the Suburban.

Concho trotted up to her and sniffed Vivian's hamper before she tossed it into the back seat.

"This isn't my idea! Since Isabela can't go, she asked me to entertain you. I told her no, but she wouldn't listen."

"If you were Isabela, you'd be more enthusiastic," he teased huskily. "What about Miguelito?"

"He's watching cartoons and keeping Isabela company because he feels sorry for her."

"Nice kid."

"He has a soft heart."

Cash thumped the Suburban with his open hand. "So, it's off to the beach house, then. Just the two of us?"

His green eyes brightened as he studied her mouth and then the rest of her body with an intensity that caused her to blush.

"No. That's tomorrow…when she's better. Isabela planned a trip to Uxmal, a picnic, and a visit to a cave with an underground swimming pool."

"I'd rather go to the beach with my very own Aphrodite."

Nodding toward Eusebio, she glared mutinously at Cash. "You'd better behave. She has spies everywhere."

"Good thing they don't speak English."

"They understand body language."

"Body language," he repeated, his gaze drifting over her again.

"Would you quit?"

"To the beach house," he said, his tone changing. "I'll be a good boy and sketch. Then I'll have a head full of ideas by tomorrow…to share with Isabela."

"So, you really intend to work?"

"What other intentions do you suspect me of?" His amused-looking eyes were wide and sparkly beneath dense black lashes.

"Work. That sounds nice and safe."

"Nice? Safe? Unless you decide to strip again or seduce me into another torrid kiss." His lips moved closer as if to tempt her.

She jumped back. "This isn't going to work—"

Concho whined.

"Truce! White flag!" Cash grabbed a white bath sheet out of her hamper and waved it at her. His eyes flicked over her body again so hotly she feared he could see through tightly woven white cotton.

"Okay."

When their bags, groceries, drinks and towels were stuffed into the back, Eusebio banged the cargo doors shut, then went up to the front of the car and lifted the hood.

"And don't forget your swimsuit," Cash reminded her. "The red bikini. I have a hankering to see you *in* it. It's in—"

"I know where it is," she snapped, grabbing the white towel from him and slinging it back into her hamper.

"I could get it for you. I mean, if you don't want to return to the scene of our crime."

"I'll get it myself!"

Concho caught the emotion in her statement and barked excitedly.

Feeling self-conscious because she was afraid Cash would watch her, which was exactly what he did, she stomped off toward the pool house with Concho bounding across the lawn beside her.

Dios! She could feel Cash's eyes burning her butt the whole way.

The cutest butt in Mérida, he'd said.

She whirled. Yes, indeedy, his alert tiger gaze was glued to her backside. He laughed and lowered his gaze.

But Eusebio didn't. The chauffeur's expression was too keen and speculative for her liking.

Behind Vivian, the glittering green Caribbean stretched to a cloudless horizon. Not that Cash was looking at the aqua sea or admiring the town of Progreso, which he had come to see.

Hell, he had eyes only for *her*. With the sea breeze in her red hair and the white *huipil* blowing about her breasts, and her skirt whipping her hips and slim legs, Vivian was beautiful. But it wasn't just her beauty that got to him. It was the way her cheeks brightened every time he touched her or glanced at her. Her every blush, her every downcast glance to hide her true feelings made him remember their kiss. No one had ever been so responsive to him.

He was glad chance had forced her to come with him.

Behind her, waves rolled lazily up to the beach. In the distance a few swimmers splashed in the surf. The dense warm air, cooler here than in the city, smelled of salt, and mariachi music drifted from an open-air bar. The beach town had a laid-back feel.

He didn't want to sketch. He wanted to romance her, to get to know her slowly, to talk over beers and fried fish, to dance together afterward.

If only he wasn't so acutely aware of the dark figure leaning against the hood of Isabela's parked Suburban, watching them as they strolled the promenade along the beach.

"Before the hurricane, Isabela used to let Miguelito and me use her beach house anytime." Vivian's blue eyes sparkled.

Cash frowned with annoyance as he glanced from Vivian to the chauffeur. He felt increasingly guilty about not feeling more for Isabela—the last thing he wanted to talk about was her.

"Can't we talk about something else?" he said. "I wanted to know about the *henequen* plantations we passed getting here, but, no, all you would talk about, the entire twenty-two-mile drive to this beach, was perfect Isabela. Surely no living mortal is as perfect as you describe her.''

"Oh, but she is,'' Vivian gushed.

"Then why are you so anxious to leave her and Mexico?''

"Not because she hasn't been incredibly generous to me and to Miguelito. I just need to find myself. To do my own thing.''

"Are you lost?''

She ran her hand through her hair and turned away. "Maybe 'homesick' is a better word. Or 'unchallenged.'''

"How about 'unfulfilled'?''

She blushed at the charged innuendo. "When I came down here, it was to study for three months. I thought I would finish my degree before I married. Maybe work a while. But here I am—trapped by fate and bad judgment.''

"Because you're a dedicated mother of a darling little boy.''

"You think he's darling?'' she asked.

He looked beyond her to the four-mile-long pier the natives had had to build to reach deep water because the Yucatecan limestone shelf declined so gradually into the Caribbean.

"You chose well,'' he said, after a moment, "to put him first.''

"Back to Isabela,'' Vivian began.

"Stop—''

"I feel so guilty being here with you…when she can't be.''

He grabbed her hand and pressed her fingers inside the warmth of his. "I don't want to think about her. I'm perfectly happy here with you.''

Again she blushed as if his touch and his words gave her too much pleasure. "Me too. Which is the problem…'' She bit her lip.

He felt a warm flush of pleasure at the revelation that she liked him, and he drew her closer. The wind made her beautiful red hair ripple like a multicolored banner, the sunlight changing it from shimmering copper to auburn to honey gold and then back to copper again. Why the hell couldn't he forget seeing her naked or kissing her? Or how much fun it had been to tease her over breakfast?

"No more talk about Isabela," he whispered, letting her go but continuing to stare into her eyes.

"She's your future bride," she whispered. "And she's better to me than any sister ever could be."

"Right," he agreed in a bored tone. "But since we're here in Progreso, and she's not, maybe you wouldn't mind playing tourist guide and telling me a few things about the town."

"For instance?"

"Where the hell is everybody?" Cash pointed to the empty street and the Caribbean. "I thought Progreso was a resort like Cancún."

"It is, but on a smaller scale. Cancún is more for foreigners. This is for Mexicans."

"Hell, it's a village compared to a real Mexican beach resort," he said.

"You wouldn't say that in the summer when all of Mérida is here."

"Well, nobody's here today."

Her deep blue eyes seemed to speak to him. "Nobody but us."

Quickly she averted her eyes. "Puerto Progreso was built in the mid-nineteenth century to ship *henequen* to the rest of the world. There? Do I sound like a proper tourist guide?"

"Keep going."

"The *henequen* plants—you saw them growing—produce strong fibers that can be used in twine- and rope-making."

"I read synthetics have largely destroyed the industry." His eyes caressed her.

"Hence—Progreso is a lazy beach town."

"The hotels are so small," he said, wondering if he couldn't send Eusebio on some sort of errand.

"Intimate," she corrected. "It's the middle of the week and not yet high season. Isabela loves it here. You should see her...."

Vivian began to repeat her monologue about what a perfect wife Isabela would make.

He nodded. "But Isabela isn't here." His gaze skimmed her mouth. "You are."

She licked her lips and cast a sideways glance toward Eusebio, who was watching them.

"You don't have to use Isabela to erect a wall between us," he said.

"I would never forgive myself if I ruined her chances." She broke away from him and moved quickly toward the SUV.

Eusebio smiled, and Cash watched the way the loose, white *huipil* shivered around her waist as she ran. Her black skirt fluttered against her knees, shaping itself against her hips. Since he'd seen her naked, it wasn't hard to imagine her naked with the green Caribbean sparkling beyond her.

Botticelli's vision of Aphrodite stepping out of the sea sprang to mind. Vivian was a far more glorious depiction of Venus than the master's rendition. At least Cash thought so.

Vivian. Venus. God, what he would give to be able to rip those awful, embroidered, handmade rags from the perfection of her body.

He wanted his wife in sleek, figure-fitting, designer gowns…. In the finest jewels. She would be a queen.

Wife? The truly crazy notion slammed him like a fist to his solar plexus, and he stopped, watching her as she climbed into the SUV. Even when she hung her head out the open window and smiled at him, he stayed put.

Her white smile warmed him. But the warm quickening that that sweet little smile caused was just physical, he told himself as he began walking toward her again—just something he needed to fill his loneliness.

Why then did he feel as if his world had shifted? As if he could finally see light at the end of a tunnel instead of perpetual darkness.

He wanted *her,* not Isabela.

He wanted her despite the fact that she was a poor divorcée, a nobody. Despite the fact she scarcely had any formal education. She was a poor girl and the mother of a sweet, trusting little boy.

She was completely unacceptable to his family. What would Jake, his brother, the ambitious senator, make of her?

Hell, who gave his cold family the right to make the rules he lived by?

When Vivian beat on the side of her door like it was a drum and called to him to hurry, he felt himself in the grip of something that felt an awful lot like destiny.

Leo believed fate was stronger than human will. Cash was too rational to entertain such an idea. But what if a rational man struck a compromise with the gods?

Cash had come here for a bride. Why not Vivian?

Why the hell not?

Nine

It is strange how life goes along in a familiar pattern, and then it changes—sometimes slowly, sometimes rapidly. For Vivian that afternoon with Cash in Progreso was such a day.

One minute she was standing on the Malecón with Cash, determined to be loyal to Isabela and resist him, and in the next she was in the Suburban smiling at him until his dark face lit up and his fierce grin thrilled her to the point of insanity.

Suddenly her spirits were rocketing higher than the sun. Her loneliness and her lack of fulfillment, her desire to escape Mexico and become somebody on her own, and even her fear of what she felt for him, were all eclipsed by something grander and more mysterious.

She didn't stop smiling until he swung his tall frame into the back seat beside her. Cash asked her about her uncle and New Orleans, and she found herself talking easily about the fact she'd grown up with "two daddies." She spoke of her old interest in archaeology, and in the Mayans, and of her more recent work with the Mayan villagers. She said maybe on their way home they could stop at one of the villages where she worked and he could meet the people.

"You'd do that—even if I ruined your reputation in the market?"

She went still for a moment. Then she told him about Mexico and how a thousand years of western civilization was but a thin veneer on top of ancient traditions.

"So, the Mexican is never what you think he is or what he says he is," she said in her best schoolteacher voice.

Cash told her he wanted more than anything to meet her Mayan students. He suggested that perhaps she had a vocation for social work, and she said she found satisfaction in helping others, especially in teaching.

"I enjoy working with them," she said as they drove down the sandy lanes of the town.

He told her of his own life. He'd been a lonely little boy who'd grown up motherless in vast houses. He'd known the servants better than he'd known his own father. Not that his father had been cruel; he'd simply been consumed by making money. Eagerly she listened as Cash told her about the projects he had built in Paris, Rome, London, and most recently Florence, of the proposal he'd lost in Manhattan.

When they'd driven through the narrow back streets of the town as well as the main street along the ocean, she said, "Is there anything else you need to do or see?"

He stared at her and said, "Most definitely."

She blushed. "Before we go to the beach house, I want to take you shopping at a store and the market."

"I'm not much of a shopper," Cash said. "Besides, because of you, I bought everybody I know hats—that are probably too small."

She laughed. "I'll shop, you watch."

He followed her into an open-air market and then to a small *tienda* across the street where she bought flowers and two disposable cameras. No sooner were they at Isabela's beach house—built on three levels so it wouldn't sprawl across the sandy lot—than she spread their picnic things out on a table in the back courtyard and began to take pictures of everything. First, she had to get shots of a pair of pink flamingos in the back gardens. Then she captured numerous angles of Isabela's ruined mansion, but last and most lingeringly of all, she took pictures of him.

"Why the camera?" he demanded between bites of banana when she said "smile." He was on a break between sketches of the cantilevered pavilions over the pool, so he humored her with silly faces and big grins.

"Pictures capture time. They help me remember special moments," she said. "And pictures tell stories."

He jumped up and grabbed the camera from her. "Mind if I capture a precious memory or two?"

She held up her hands, and he snapped a picture of her. Then she blushed, and he knelt and took five or six more. When she was thoroughly embarrassed, he seized her by the hand and led her over to Eusebio and asked the chauffeur to photograph them together.

Later, after he'd sketched the outside, she unlocked the house and they climbed the stairs to the living and dining areas as well as the master bedroom, which were all on the top level.

"Since salt corrodes metal and Sheetrock is so absorbent, Isabela's father used concrete and stone as the primary materials in the construction," she said, as if he couldn't see this for himself.

The second level housed four more bedrooms, with pavilions at each end of the house cantilevered like balconies over the pool. The glass had been blown out of all the windows; the rooms were vacant shells.

"Hurricanes are terrible here," she said as they made their way through the hauntingly exquisite ruin. "Violent and unpredictable."

"A force of nature. Like Mexico's ancient gods," he said huskily as they descended to the lower level.

"When I am done," he said softly, "the house will be more beautiful than before."

Excited and inspired, whether by her or by the place, he sat down on a bottom stair and began to draw. She watched him, fascinated as his dark hand skimmed over sheets of paper leaving deft, dramatic black lines. But finally the lure of the green water was too much. The sun would soon be down and her chance to swim lost, so she left him to put her suit on and go for a dip.

Shedding her *huipil* and black skirt on the beach and exposing the red bikini underneath, she walked to the water's edge. Never before had the wet sand beneath her toes felt so silky and warm. She scrunched her toes into it. Glancing back at the house she caught Cash watching her from one of the pavilions.

Her body heated, remembering as bodies do, the wild, heady pleasure of his mouth on hers, the exact taste and texture of his tongue sliding inside her lips, the feel of his callused fingers on her skin as his arms wrapped around her. Other physical memories, like the lava heat of his body against hers, bombarded her.

Isabela, why did you make me come here?

Vivian was weak. She couldn't look at him without remembering seeing him naked, without remembering his kisses. To distract herself she splashed into the waves and swam back and forth in the warm salty sea.

Swimming in those clear waters was pure bliss. It was as if she became the sea. She swam for at least thirty minutes before she saw him running across the beach toward the water, wearing his swimsuit. He was dark, muscular and shapely—perfect. He plunged into the surf and swam toward her, his strong, brown arms slicing the water with remarkable skill. She couldn't help being impressed by the fact he was a powerful swimmer.

"Hi," she said when he reached her and stood up, shaking himself like an overgrown puppy. "You're supposed to be working."

"I saw you out here and couldn't resist temptation."

When his eyes lingered on her bikini top, she felt like stripping it off and swimming naked. On that thought, she swam away from him again, but he chased after her, catching her easily, grabbing her by the ankle and then slowing his strokes to match hers.

They swam for a long time, both above the water and beneath it, like two dolphins cavorting. When she'd had enough, she stood up. Without a word she began strolling languidly toward shore.

He paddled up behind her and splashed her to get her attention. She whirled and pretended to be annoyed, but he merely grinned and splashed her again. When he wouldn't stop, she screamed, but he just splashed her harder. The raucous water fight that ensued left them breathless with laughter.

Only when she called for a truce did he quit. For a moment they stood breathing heavily in the sunlight, their wet bodies glistening, each too aware of the forbidden excitement being together caused.

"The less you wear, the better you look," he said.

"Don't ruin everything—"

"If you took off your top, you'd look like Aphrodite coming out of the sea."

To tempt him, she fingered the strap of her bikini top.

Then, as if he had rights he didn't have, he moved toward her and touched her cheek with his fingertips. Next he ran his thumb over her lips. She drew his thumb into her mouth and sucked on it. He was warm, as warm as the salty sea.

His hand went lower, along the line of her cheek, down her throat, feeling its way along the supple curve of her shoulder, down to the strap of her bikini, which he lowered over her arm.

"I want to kiss you again so much," he said in a husky tone. His eyes grew tender. "And I don't want to ever stop."

Even before he spoke, she could feel her body taking charge. It remembered every thrill she'd experienced with him—from his striptease in the pool house to his kiss in the oven-like market.

"If you were Isabela, I'd kiss you," he said.

"But I'm not. So a kiss isn't allowed."

"Says who?"

She couldn't quit staring at his wide shoulders or at his mouth.

Any more than he could stop staring at hers. "If you were Isabela, you'd let me," he whispered, moving closer, lifting the chain from her throat. "Very pretty."

"A gift from Isabela. Speaking of Isabela, she's probably been calling me on my cell phone."

"I want you," he said baldly.

"But you'll marry *her*. And Eusebio might be—"

"To hell with them. What about us?"

"This morning we made a plan—"

"Before I realized how deeply I felt about you."

"I don't believe you."

"Believe this, then."

She started to protest, but Cash pulled her down into the surf and kissed her before she could argue. Then her body took over, and the warm water rushed over them. She kissed him back, this time with less resistance.

In the market he'd broken down the walls and defenses that had taken her years to erect. As the surf broke over them, rocking their bodies together, she felt overrun, and she no longer had the presence of mind to care. Her feelings for Cash were so sweet and wickedly wild and all-consuming, it was impossible to think of Isabela.

"Cash—" Her hands fisted against his dark, furred chest.

He was huge, his dark handsomeness startling. Broad shoulders narrowed to a lean waist. His legs and arms felt like they were made of muscle. She'd never been so close to such a virile, attractive man. And he was successful on a world-class scale. When they were together he treated her like an equal. But they weren't equals. Not in the real world. She was playing with fire, and yet being with him like this was so wonderful, she couldn't stop herself from opening her mouth and melting against him.

Something outside her took over and she welcomed his tongue inside her mouth, tasting salt and him with an eagerness that stunned her. Lying in the surf, the water brushed her thighs and breasts into him. Their swirling bodies went beneath the waves, and she felt his hands touching her everywhere.

She came up from the surf gasping and laughing, all her will to fight gone because of the delight her body found in his. He pulled her back into his arms and kissed her again.

I can make you happy, she thought as his mouth closed over hers and more warm waves licked them. *Happier than you've ever been.*

But after that? What would happen after that? Passion didn't last.

And there was Isabela. Darling Isabela.

"This is wrong," Vivian said. "Isabela's done a lot for me. I owe her more than betrayal." She stood up.

He lunged for her slim ankle, but she hopped out of his clutches. "If she really loved you, wouldn't she understand that things like this happen?"

"I don't want to try to explain that to her. I don't want to hurt her. She's been so wonderful to me."

"Please—no more sermons about how perfect she is."

"You're right." Vivian smoothed her dripping hair back out of her eyes. The sky toward Mérida was darkening. She frowned.

"Okay," she said. "See that big black cloud? It's probably going to rain soon. Why don't we dry off and dress. If you're hungry, I know a great fish restaurant in town where they fry the fish whole. Or we can just head home—I wouldn't want Isabela to worry."

"What about our picnic supper?"

"Beer and music would be better." *And other people to take my mind off Cash.*

"You're afraid to be here alone with me after the sun goes down."

Without looking at him, she said, "Sometimes it's scary the way you can read my mind."

"That's not what scares you."

She felt a sweet, warm tightening somewhere in her midsection. *Dear Lord, I want him so badly.* She swallowed. "We'd better hurry. I really think it might rain," she said.

He stared past her at the mass of clouds. "So what if it does?"

"I told you—I don't want to be late. I don't want Isabela to worry."

"This is our day. Our one day together." Without saying more, he drew her hands to his mouth. He kissed each open palm so lingeringly that she shivered. He lifted his tousled black head. "Is it so wrong for us to enjoy each other?" His beautiful voice was strange and hoarse, and he seemed so earnest, so honest. Being with him did feel wonderful on many levels. Was it wrong?

Lowering his head, he kissed her wrists, and heat washed her. She swallowed again, still not knowing what to say or do because her mind and conscience dictated one thing and her heart and body something completely different.

She let out a breath and inhaled another. She should stop him, but his lips nibbling higher and higher up her arms caused silky tantalizing sensations to pulsate inside her, sensations that were too delicious to resist.

Finally, Vivian felt a fat raindrop hit her toe. More spattered onto the sand around them. Thunder crashed.

In a daze she jerked her hands loose from his. She'd resisted every man until him. What in the world was happening to her?

Somehow she found her voice. "I think we'd better make a run for it."

Ten

Brows knitted, Vivian stared at the slashing windshield wipers. She felt desperate to get home before she gave in to the powerful feelings Cash aroused, but the storm was getting worse. Maybe the ancient Mexican gods weren't on her side after all.

Despite the rain, Cash had convinced her to stop for dinner on the way home. The little beachside café had been too romantic to believe, and if the sky hadn't darkened to an ominous shade of gray, they might have stayed and danced to the band for hours. Instead of dancing, they'd decided to head back to Isabela's before the storm got worse, but the torrential downpour had begun before they were halfway to Mérida.

Black rain now swept across the narrow, red dirt road that was lined on either side by whitewashed rustic walls and small pastel-colored houses. Fierce tornadic gusts tossed broken fanlike leaves and palm fronds everywhere. Soon it was all but impossible to see much of the Mayan village where Vivian had intended to stop earlier.

Coconuts torn out of trees rolled down the road on all sides of them like loose bowling balls. From time to time the SUV crunched one under its big tires.

"Isabela isn't going to believe this storm—" Vivian was jabbing at her cell phone. "Everytime I dial her, I get a busy signal."

"This is like a hurricane. You aren't going to get a signal until the storm blows itself out," Cash said. "Relax."

"We should have skipped dinner."

"Dinner was great! I never ate better fish anywhere. Even if the cook did leave the eyes when I told him not to, and that damn fish watched me and made me feel worse than a cannibal."

His easy conversation helped take her mind off the storm.

At that moment twin bolts of blue-white lightning slammed into the jungle on either side of the narrow road, and she screamed.

"Sorry." She clamped fingers over her mouth as high winds buffeted the SUV, causing it to swerve. Eusebio hunched over the wheel, straining to see into the wild wet dark.

"Maybe we should stop and wait it out," Cash suggested.

"No, this can't last long."

But it did. Sheets of water kept coming. When they were in the middle of the jungle village, all the streetlights went out. Other than the glow from the stunted bright cones of their headlights, they were in total darkness.

Suddenly a pig flew out of nowhere. Eusebio slammed on the brakes. A vicious gust hammered the side of the SUV, and the vehicle skidded in the slick mud. As a white stone wall loomed in front of them, the pig squealed, scrambled over it and vanished into a clump of catalpa trees. Eusebio yanked the steering wheel to the right.

Cash said, "Get down." When she didn't, he pulled Vivian into his arms and threw her onto the seat, lowering himself protectively over her. When she struggled, his strong hands held the back of her head against his chest.

Instead of hitting the wall head-on, the vehicle's sides scraped trees and the wall before the engine sputtered and died.

"Are you okay?" Cash asked, sitting up a little, stroking her hair.

They'd had a wreck, yet she felt safe—she was in his arms, inhaling his clean male scent, and he was concerned about her.

"Just get off me and I'll be fine," she snapped, still trying to fight her vulnerability to him.

His large, wonderfully sensitive hands touched her everywhere as if to reassure himself she really was all right—her brow, her nose, her lips, her neck, her arms and then down her spine.

In the front seat, Eusebio tried to start the SUV again, not that Vivian was wholly conscious of the chauffeur's activities. She couldn't think with Cash's arms around her.

"I'm fine," she muttered fiercely, pushing at him.

"Right," he whispered, letting her go.

Neither looked at the other. She clenched her fingers together in her lap. He unbuckled his seat belt and leaned forward to advise Eusebio as to how to start the engine. When it wouldn't start, the three of them sat in silence as the rain pounded the vehicle.

"What are we going to do?" she whispered.

"We wait," Cash replied.

Alone? Together? For how long? She didn't ask.

It wasn't long before the rain lessened and they saw movement in the jungle. Then an army of brown-skinned people appeared out of nowhere cowering under umbrellas, *rebozos* and ponchos. Fists beat on the windows, so Vivian cracked her door open and found herself staring at a young man with a narrow face and thin mustache.

"Huicho!" she cried, delighted to recognize somebody.

"I know this truck yours." He beamed at them, happy to see her as well as her rich gringo friend who'd bought so many hats. "Come out. *Mi casa es su casa.*"

Looking shaken, Eusebio said he knew a mechanic and would go for help. Before Vivian could argue, he vanished.

Huicho told her to wait. Then he brought heavy rain ponchos and led Vivian and Cash down a narrow lane lined with huts and dense tropical vegetation.

"You are lucky. A tenant of mine just moved out of my guest house," Huicho said, stopping in front of a hut and shoving the bright blue front door open. "You can stay with us for the night. Very private."

"We won't be staying for the whole night," Vivian said, her blood heating at the mere thought. "Eusebio will have us on our way long before—"

"You didn't see the front end of your truck." Huicho made a grim face. "The road ahead is like a river."

Vivian's heart sank. "Isabela…"

Soon they were across the threshold, and it was warm and dry. His children ran and lined up against the far wall, hiding their faces from their guests and giggling. A wealth of candles lit the tiny room. Lupe, his wife, brushed strands of hair out of her eyes and rushed up to greet them.

She smiled at Vivian and nodded shyly toward Cash. "I make your special friend something to eat, no?"

"We already ate. Please just show us the guest house," Cash said, "and we won't bother you for more."

Vivian stayed with Lupe and the children while Huicho showed Cash the small house behind his own cottage. When the men returned, Cash told Vivian the guest house would do nicely.

Vivian averted her eyes, and when Lupe insisted on serving them black *zapotes*, Vivian seized having a snack as an excuse to put off being in a room alone with Cash.

Black *zapotes* were a lot like giant prunes, and Lupe had removed their skins and seeds and mashed them in sugar. As always, Vivian found them to be a delicious treat. Still, she couldn't stop thinking about the night ahead.

After eating more than his share and complimenting Lupe extravagantly, Cash sat down with Huicho. To Vivian's alarm, the two men began arm wrestling and bolting shots of tequila.

Vivian begged Cash to quit, but he merely lifted his shot glass and toasted her.

"You aren't used to tequila," she said under her breath.

He laughed and lifted his shot glass toward her again.

The more the two men drank, the more they laughed and looked warmly at the women.

"If you drink any more, you'll be as drunk as a skunk," Vivian finally said.

When Huicho was about to pour Cash still another shot, Cash eyed Vivian, put his hand over the bottle and shook his head.

"My woman says no," Cash said, flashing her a grin.

Huicho nodded, eyeing Vivian with new appreciation. No doubt he was remembering the kiss in the market. Vivian was so mad she wanted to kick Cash.

Lupe smiled at them shyly and dashed out to the guest house to make it ready for them. A few minutes later when Cash led Vivian inside the little cottage, fresh lilies and hibiscus blossoms graced a rustic table, along with a bottle of tequila for Cash. White towels and dry clothes for both of them had been laid on the double bed draped with mosquito netting.

A bare bulb hung over the table, but with the electricity out, the flickering candle on the window ledge was their only source of light. A plastic curtain hung in a doorway to give privacy to the bathroom.

"Running water!" Cash said.

"All yours for the night," Lupe said with one of her quick smiles before leaving them.

"They're certainly friendly." Cash shut the door, his eyes burning her face and her body.

Vivian rushed to the door that led to the courtyard and opened it. "I work with them every week. Lupe is one of my best students. I've taught her to use a sewing machine, and she now teaches others." Vivian paused breathlessly. "I don't know what they must be thinking. This door stays open."

"They think our tank rammed into their wall."

"Why did you drink so much?" she asked, changing the subject.

"Why do you care so much?"

"I think you know."

"I'm not going to force you—if that's what you think. Or if that's what you secretly desire...."

"How dare you suggest—"

"I dare," he growled. "Why do only you get to accuse me?"

Furious, she began to pace, and then so did he, each careful to avoid the other. By American standards the room was bare. There was no television, no books, no magazines.

When Vivian ripped off her rain poncho, Cash's dark eyes grew more avid and hot. She realized her wet, clinging *huipil* and skirt were probably plastered to her breasts and hips, so she grabbed her poncho and held it up between them.

He laughed. Glancing at her watch impatiently, she realized how early it was.

"Calm down," he said.

"With you drunk and watching me with those tiger eyes of yours?"

"Hey, I'm not going to pounce you. Not unless you want me to."

"Oh, when will Eusebio return? And how will he know where we are?" In despair she plopped onto one edge of the bed.

"I wouldn't count on him for much. It looks like I'm your entertainment center," Cash said, weaving a little as he fell backward beside her, but on the opposite end of the bed.

She bolted off the bed.

"Would you like a soda or something?" he said, his tone low and casual. "I think I saw a case in Huicho's house."

"Yes."

"Anything to get me out of here?" His face lit with a savage grin.

"Yes. Yes. Yes."

"Okay. Okay. Okay," he said, amused.

"This whole situation is impossible," she added.

"Not if you change your attitude."

"This room is too small."

"Intimate," he countered.

"The soda—remember? You were going!"

"Right."

When he stomped out into the pouring rain, she eyed the double bed nervously. She hadn't even begun to relax before he was back with her soda.

As if he felt perfectly comfortable—and why wouldn't he after all he'd drunk—he sat at the table, leaned back in the chair, his long legs sprawling, and poured himself another shot of tequila, which he lifted in a mock salute to her.

"Don't be so insolent." Her forehead crinkling, she backed away from him until her spine hit the window ledge.

When he lifted his brows and saluted her again, the air between them crackled with electricity.

"This isn't working," she said. "I can't do this."

"Okay."

This whole thing was making her crazy. She was afraid. So afraid. Why? Why was she so scared of being alone with him?

Pursing her lips, she drank her soda in silence. Behind her the cool rain streamed in unending torrents into the courtyard outside, which was now six inches deep with water. She wished it would stop.

"I have to get out of here," she said.

"Ever heard the word 'destiny'?"

"Just be quiet."

Before she was half done with her soda, her cell phone

rang. Her purse was sitting on a low table near the door. When they both rushed to get it, they bumped into each other. He grabbed the strap of her purse before she could reach it. Rocking back on his heels, he swept her a courtly bow and held the purse out to her.

Trembling with rage, at least she told herself it was rage, she snatched it from him. When she couldn't open it, he grabbed it back and yanked the zipper open for her. She reached inside and retrieved her cell phone.

"Isabela?" she gasped.

"Why are you breathless?"

Vivian glared up at Cash, whose tall, wide-shouldered body loomed over her. Her entire body was quivering. "No reason," she replied.

"I've been calling you and calling you."

"Me too."

"How's Cash?"

A single glance his way, and her heartbeat picked up speed. "F-fine."

"You sound funny," Isabela observed.

Cash smiled.

She felt a strange heat climbing her limbs until it spread throughout her entire body. "He's j-just…just fine."

"Never better," he drawled, lifting his tequila toward her. "Tell her hello."

"Where—?" Isabela's voice died.

"Oh, Isabela, we broke down. But Eusebio will have things fixed in no time. He's gone to find a mechanic."

"Don't count on it. He's probably drunk. Where are you?"

Vivian eyed Cash again. His beaming face wore an inebriated smile. Through gritted teeth, she said the name of the village.

"I'll send a cab," Isabela said.

Before Vivian could give her directions, a flash of lightning whitened the room and the cell phone went dead. Frantically, she tried to call Isabela back while Cash stared at her, smiling charmingly. She jabbed at the buttons, but all she could get was that maddening busy signal.

"Quit watching me and quit smiling at me," she yelled at Cash, throwing the phone at the bed in frustration.

"You're wet and cold," he said. "No wonder you're so grumpy." He stood up.

"If I'm grumpy, it's your fault. And...and stay right where you are."

"And if I'm in a good mood, whose fault is that?" he demanded silkily.

"Not mine! You're drunk!"

"Maybe a warm shower would make you feel better?"

With you out here drinking tequila? Not in a million years.

"I could ask Huicho if there's a phone in the village," Cash said in a reasonable, helpful tone that maddened her all the more.

"There is, but with our rotten luck, it's out."

"I'll check and see anyway."

"Great!"

"Anything to get rid of me?" He smiled.

She glared.

"Take a shower while I'm gone. And don't use up all the hot water."

"What makes you so sure there is any?"

"Ah...the delights of sharing authentic Mexico with you. This could be fun you know—if you'd loosen up."

Too much fun. She clasped her arms around herself. "Go."

"If you're too chicken to shower, why don't you just get into bed?"

"Bed?" Her mouse voice was back. Nevertheless, the word *bed* hung heavily between them.

"And what will you do? Strip for me? Like you did before? And then hop in too? Nothing would surprise me from you."

He scowled and crossed his arms over his chest. "Nothing is what I'll do. Understand? I won't do a damn thing. I like you and respect you. I don't want to hurt Isabela any more than you do. I'm not some oversexed maniac, you know.''

"I can't forget how you ripped off that sheet."

"I was being gallant. I won't force you—ever." Furious, he dove through the open doorway. Boots sloshing in the deep water, he vanished into the roaring storm.

Good! She was glad he was mad.

But no sooner was he gone than a gust of wind blew the candle out and she was all alone in the dark. Instantly she wished him back.

For a while she sat in the dark and listened to the storm, but that only increased her agitation. She didn't remember where the matches were or if there were any, and without him to distract her she became aware of the buzzing of mosquitoes and the incessant pouring of the rain on the tiles outside.

In the courtyard she heard racing footsteps. Then a girl laughed shyly, and a boy said something tender—young lovers taking shelter under an eave. Vivian felt a strange twinge in the area near her heart...and longed for Cash.

The couple's gentle voices were followed by increasingly torrid kisses and then by more animalistic pantings and ardent caresses. A shutter began to bang in the rhythm of lovemaking. Vivian thought of Cash and began to ache.

Hardly knowing what she did, her hand ran down her throat over her breast. With a shivery sigh she closed her eyes and imagined Cash touching her. Then her hand traced lower, to her stomach and then still lower, to her hip, and finally between her legs. The shutter banged harder. Only when she moaned did she come to her senses and jerk her hand away. She bit her knuckles and tried not to listen to the lovers, tried not to want a man who could never be hers.

Finally she remembered she did have matches—in her purse. Stumbling across the room, she dug them out. Still shaking, she relit the candle and leaned against the wall.

When Cash still didn't return, she took the fresh clothes and towels and the burning candle into the bathroom and stripped. To her surprise, the water from the nozzle felt warm and delicious against her naked skin. Lathering her hair, she reveled in the soft suds running down over her body. She was covered in soap when her phone rang again.

Then the ringing stopped abruptly. She started when she heard a low, male voice say, "Isabela." When she strained closer to the curtain to hear what else he said, something wet and slimy skittered across her bare toe.

She looked down into huge, liquid, equally-terrified, black eyes—reptilian eyes. Jumping, she screamed and screamed.

"Cash! It's going to bite me! It's—"

The thing hopped as frantically as she, bouncing into her leg. She grabbed the shower curtain and ripped it off. The next thing she knew she was out of the shower and Cash was in the bathroom, his arms wrapped around her sudsy body. She was naked, wet and slippery, and soon his jeans and white shirt were soaked. She climbed him anyway, wrapping her legs around his waist and hanging on for dear life.

"What the hell." Then he looked down and grinned at the tiny monster. "Shh. It's just a little toad. Nothing to be afraid of, darling," he said gently.

Darling. The word registered even though she wished it hadn't.

"Get him out of here!" Vivian shrieked, wrapping her legs around him even more tightly. "Get me out of here!"

Carrying her, Cash stomped out of the shower dripping puddles all over the tile floor. Finally, she let go of him and ran naked to the bed, leaving Cash to return and deal with the odious reptile.

She wrapped herself in the sarape that had been thrown over the bed. "Did you kill it yet?"

"I can't get him," he said when he came out of the bathroom. "You scared him too badly. He's hiding under a wooden slat and won't come out. And I don't blame him."

"Don't you dare take his side. What will I do? I can't go back in there if he's there."

Cash was clipping the shower curtain back onto the rod. "Then stay put!"

"But I've got soap all over me."

"He won't hurt you, you know. He's cute."

"Cute?"

"Come look at him."

She tiptoed closer. "I'm not so good with reptiles."

He laughed. "A toad is an amphibian—not a reptile."

Who cared what the monster was? Clutching the serape tighter, she raced past him back to the bathroom. Yanking the curtain shut, she summoned her courage and searched for the toad. He was curled into a little ball and almost completely hidden under the wooden slat. He was a tiny, big-eyed little thing. He did look terrified of her.

Not that she was about to sympathize with a reptile or an amphibian, or whatever the horrible thing was.

She stuck the tip of her toe onto the first wooden slat. When he didn't jump her, she edged more deeply into the cubicle and turned on the shower. With a sigh, she finished rinsing her hair and her body in the warm downpour before the hot water ran out. After drying herself off, she ventured out of the bathroom swaddled in towels.

"Hey—did you leave me a towel?"

"One."

"You were right about the phone," he said. "The lines are down. Mind if I shower?"

Even though she did, she shook her head. "But you were right about the hot water. I used it all."

He gave her a look that softened the expression on his dark face even though his eyes grew brilliant. "Maybe you did us both a favor."

When Cash took his icy shower, yelping most dramatically at the water's temperature, she got into bed. Even though he was behind the curtain, she could see the dark silhouette of his big body. Again her hand drifted over her body, and it was too easy to imagine him touching her. She yanked her hand above the sheets and stared miserably.

She shouldn't have taken the candle in there, she realized. She shouldn't watch him now...but she couldn't stop herself.

The water was turned off and he emerged, his narrow hips wrapped in the diminutive white towel she'd left him. Shivering, she pulled the sheets up to her throat. His bronzed, muscular, goose-bump-covered body raised gooseflesh on her and left her slightly breathless.

The wind rose and beat against the roof. Anticipation made her tremble and then go taut. When he stopped and stared down at her body outlined by the sheets, her pulse beat in her throat.

Dios. Soon he would get into bed. And then—

But he didn't approach the bed. Instead, he pivoted and went back into the bathroom, where he blew out the candle. She gripped the sheets breathlessly above her breasts until he emerged. He moved about. Fabric rustled. What was he doing?

Closing her eyes, she lay there waiting, wondering, and feeling so hot she was afraid she'd burn up.

To her surprise, she heard a sound at the door.

"I'll be back later," he whispered softly.

She sat up, not caring that the sheets fell from her body. "Where are you going?"

"You don't want me here. That much is clear. Go to sleep."

"But...but you're wrong," she said.

Not that he heard her. He was already out the door, sloshing noisily through the deep water again and quickly disappearing in the darkness. When all sounds of him vanished, she'd never felt so alone. She wanted him back.

She wanted him.

Wind and rain slashed the trees. Even so, there were jungle sounds—shouts, shrieks, screeches, howls, hoots. She imagined reptiles—huge snakes, their thick coils luridly colored.

For what seemed like hours, she lay in the bed awake, tossing and turning, listening for his footsteps outside.

The phone rang once, only to die before she could get to it.

"Oh, Cash." Her heart pounded in fright as she imagined his fatal encounter with a big cat, or maybe a snake or a crocodile that tore him to pieces.

An animal screamed, and her stomach knotted. She sat up, brushing hot wetness from her cheeks. She'd been so mean to him. Why had she said such awful things?

If only…

Finally, she became so exhausted she sank into a nightmarish sleep, full of large reptiles, from which she didn't awaken until dawn. When she blinked, glorious streamers of pink light streaked the whitewashed walls. The rain had stopped, and the jungle was mercifully silent.

The early-morning air held a chill but she felt warm and safe, so safe and so warm, and at peace as she hadn't in years. She stirred lazily, and when she did, her fingers brushed hot, solid, male muscle. Idly she traced the shape of a steely limb, savoring every sensation, before realizing it was a man's arm draped proprietorially across her waist.

Her eyes flew open. She saw a wall of bronze—broad shoulders and a dark, furred chest. She smelled his clean man scent.

"Cash…"

"Good morning," he said, his dark eyes alight and tender.

"You're alive." Her smile was brilliant. "You came back. The big reptiles—I mean amphibians—didn't eat you."

"Will miracles never cease? You're glad to see me."

Vivian felt alive and very pleased he was there. "Don't tease. I was terrible to you. I'm sorry. I'm sorry."

"It's okay."

"How long have you been back?"

"A while. I couldn't find Eusebio, so I tried to sleep in the

Suburban. When the rain died down a little, I decided to check on you. You were having a nightmare."

Her voice caught. "I nearly went out of my mind."

"Me too. I wanted to be here with you."

She swallowed.

"Better now?" he drawled as his hand slid down her back.

"Oh, Cash," she breathed, throwing her arms around him. Suddenly she was too aware of her naked body snugged against his, of her nipples against his chest.

"This is where I've wanted you since I first saw you, Aphrodite."

She opened her eyes again and saw that his face was flushed and his eyes dark with desire. She knew that look, and she reveled in it. Her fear for him last night had taught her how much she desired him.

He started to get up, but she ran her hands through his long, black hair, smiling when he shuddered with delight. Time seemed to stop. She closed her eyes and pressed her body into his.

He went still, and for a long time she was afraid nothing would happen. Then she slid her body against his, and his breathing grew even raspier.

"You're sure about this?"

She nodded. Her body was wrapped by his. What guilt she felt was overpowered by her desire and the rightness she felt of belonging to him. Cash was special. She didn't know why. He just was. She had to have him. If she didn't, she'd regret it the rest of her life.

His fingers touched her mouth and then brushed her cheek. She caught his hand and kissed his fingertips, one by one, tasting them, tasting him.

"I'm just so glad you're alive," she said.

"The danger was all in your imagination," he said.

Rolling on top of him, she straddled his lean, taut body. It was strange that she felt no shyness, that she felt so natural with him. Lowering her head, she started kissing him, letting her tongue lave his throat, his washboard middle, his hard arms.

What if he were in the belly of a snake at this very moment? She was just so thrilled he was alive, so sure of her feelings for him that all doubt vanished.

"I—I can't wait much longer," he muttered, stopping a moment to fumble with a plastic wrapper. He was putting on a condom to protect her, she realized. When he was done, she sighed as his hands closed around her buttocks. Lifting her and positioning her, he thrust upward, causing her to gasp a little when she felt him inside of her. He was hard, hot and male. He made her feel complete.

She ran her hands over his arms. Her nipples brushed against his chest. His warm mouth nuzzled her ear.

Then he began to move his body against hers, and she clutched his long black hair and whispered, "Don't stop. Don't ever ever stop."

"You're heaven," he murmured. "I never thought I could feel like this again."

"It's the same for me."

For a long moment he stared into her eyes. She felt so safe, so incredibly safe with him. Then he began to move faster and faster, and it seemed to her they'd always been lovers and would always be lovers. Her feelings mounted, and her world spun crazily out of control. She was on fire, exploding, and still he kept moving inside her, causing the explosions to go on and on until she felt like she was fainting and dying, and yet, letting go of needs and hungers that always before had terrified her.

Not with him. She wasn't afraid with him. He was different—kind, responsible, wonderful.

He stopped, resting for a while. Then he began again, grabbing her hips hard and thrusting with such powerful force that she came again and again. Afterward, she went limp and began to weep, clinging to his neck.

She placed her head beside his on the pillow and he brushed

her damp hair out of her eyes. "It isn't over. Not nearly," he murmured, whispering love words in languages she did not understand.

"I dreamed about this," she said. "The first night…that's why I decided to swim. Then you had to go and take off your clothes. And now here we are just like in my dream…me on top of you."

He laughed. "It's my turn to be on top."

"I'm too tired."

"Why, love? When I'm doing all the work."

"How dare you call making love to me work?"

"Can I help it if I enjoy my work?" Laughing, he rolled them over and began to make love to her slowly. His lips suckled each nipple. Shuddering like a wanton, she came again and again, weeping afterward each time.

"Why are you crying?" he whispered in a deep, concerned tone.

"Does there always have to be a reason." He was too wonderful. What had she done to deserve anyone so wonderful?

"You're getting ahead of me, wild thing," he teased when she lay back down beside him, curled into a sensual, boneless puddle.

"I'm embarrassing myself, that's what I'm doing. I didn't want you to know how much I wanted you."

"I knew. I think that was always a big part of your appeal."

She wrapped her arms around him and he entered her again. "You're deliciously wet," he said.

This time he held nothing back. With a guttural cry he came, deep inside her, and she locked her legs around him and held him fast, never wanting to let him go.

Afterward, she thought maybe he would make love to her again, but he just lay there holding her, stroking her back, while she combed his beautiful black hair with her fingers.

She would have fallen asleep without a single guilty qualm, if only her cell phone hadn't rung.

She said, "Don't answer it."

"We can't hide forever," he said.

It stopped ringing, and she snuggled closer to him, but after a minute or two it rang again.

With a groan he got up. More than anything, she wanted to call him back to bed, to hold on to this precious time they'd shared.

"Hello, Isabela," he murmured casually before falling silent for a while. His deep, melodious voice grew concerned. "Yes, I'm afraid you'd better send a wrecker as well as a cab for us. Eusebio ran off last night, and the Suburban won't start. Yes, yes, we're fine...don't worry about us. She's fine."

Vivian cringed guiltily.

"I'll put her on," he said, "so she can give you the necessary directions."

"No! No, I can't possibly talk to her now!" Vivian whispered urgently.

He leaned over and kissed her brow. "I'm sorry, but we can't avoid this."

When she nodded, he handed her the phone.

Vivian took the phone, which felt icy to the touch.

"Isabela, *querida*—"

Eleven

In spite of the heat in the back seat of the cab of the wrecker, Vivian's shaking hand at her throat felt cool and lifeless. Her head ached from the strain of her tense conversation with Isabela.

She turned and stared out the back window. Cash's head and broad shoulders were in her line of vision. He was working even harder than Eusebio, who had finally returned, and the other laborers to attach the Suburban to the wrecker. Every time he braced a brown hand against the sides of the vehicle and shoved, his muscles strained, causing Vivian's heart to beat strangely.

Guilt over Isabela coupled with her desire for him had her totally confused.

She needed to talk to him. She needed to sort this out.

Other than the blue sky, the dense humidity and the countryside seeming cleansed and somehow greener, there was barely any sign there had been a storm. The limestone earth had soaked up the deluge like a sponge.

She leaned forward and caught a glimpse of her flushed, wide-eyed face in the mirror. Unless she confessed, would

Isabela, who trusted her, even see? Vivian touched her cheek in wonder. Were all traces of the passion she'd felt this morning erased, at least from the surface? She knew her heart, however, would never be the same.

Vivian wiped her perspiring brow and turned away to stare at the jungle. Isabela didn't deserve to be hurt.

She felt torn too, because her feelings for Cash ran deeper than any she'd ever felt for anyone. She would never forget him. Her hands knotted the thick black fabric on her knees: No way did a divorcée who was a college dropout deserve a man like him.

Finally the men finished and Cash tipped each of them. Eusebio climbed into the wrecker's truck, and Cash slid unsmilingly into the back seat with her. Like her, he kept to his side of the cab and stared out his window, his stiff posture and the tight line of his mouth telling her he wasn't any happier with himself than she was with herself.

"I'm sorry," she whispered, once they were speeding toward the outskirts of the village. "So terribly sorry…for ruining everything."

He turned. His face was dark, his green eyes brilliant and bleak. Suddenly the quiet felt ominous in the cab.

"Will you ever forgive me?" she asked. "Will she?"

"Is that really the issue?"

She swallowed. Turning, she stared at the blur of tropical green foliage. She put her hand to her perspiring temple and felt the hammer of her pulse beneath her fingertips. She felt as dazed as a sleepwalker waking from a bad dream. And yet…

"I don't understand," she said at last.

"Don't you?"

She bit her lip again. Everything looked the same as yesterday—the dense foliage, the stone *albaradas,* these walls that had no cement, and yet the familiar village felt alien and unreal. The giant thatched huts that look liked beehives rushing past them were as quaint as ever. So were the Mayan women she taught, who were wearing their immaculate white, embroidered dresses and standing in front of their houses to wave goodbye to them as their two-vehicle parade passed.

"You want to just pretend it never happened, don't you," he said. "We never saw each other naked. We never kissed. We never told each other the stories of our lives." His voice deepened. "We never made love…. You even want to act like we don't feel the way we do."

His tension and his unhappy, shadowed eyes made her ache for the kind and gentle lover who'd been so wonderful to her in bed. But he belonged with a woman from his own class— someone richer, more accomplished and sophisticated.

"I wish it had never happened," she said.

"Damn you for that lie."

She knotted her fingers. When he reached for her hand, she pulled it behind her and held it there, keeping it balled into a tight fist.

For a while they drove in a silence that grew so thick and oppressive, she was almost glad when he spoke again.

"What are those three-foot-high metal racks over there?" he murmured, his voice astonishingly soft and deep, the husky sound sending a chill through her because it was so impersonal now.

"Over there!" he persisted gently when she stiffened, refusing to be drawn into conversation. "The ones that look like rusting bedsprings?"

When she still didn't answer, he nudged her arm. "Can't we even talk to each other about safe subjects?"

Against her will, her body responded to the warmth of his hand. Instead of showing it, however, she scooted as far from him as she could.

"The rusting bedsprings," he repeated. "What are they?"

He was driving her crazy. She wanted to ignore him. She had to ignore him. Stubbornly, she thrust her chin out and bit her lips.

"We didn't commit murder. We made love," he said. "And now—"

She didn't want to talk about now. There was no now. Better to talk about the *henequen* plantations.

"All right. All right." Her voice caught and she made a little choking sound. "That's where they used to dry the *henequen*," she mumbled, looking before lowering her head and closing her eyes. "As if you could possibly care."

"I care."

"Don't."

After that, she only spoke to him when Cash asked her a direct question about the big houses in ruins or the ancient machinery on the *henequen* plantations.

Finally, she blurted, "Quit asking me stupid, tourist questions. This is all wrong—you and me, together… Last night… Us… Trying to act like it meant something when you're supposed to marry Isabela."

"It's you I want," he said gently.

"You can't change your mind just because…"

When he wouldn't stop shaking his head, she moaned. "I'll hate me forever for ruining her chances with you."

"Why? It just happened. You came into my bedroom and stripped. You were beautiful—like a dream—but it wasn't a dream. I like you as a person. You changed my life."

"Right. Blame me." She was being crazy, difficult, impossible, but she couldn't help it. Her life had turned upside down, and she didn't know what to do about it.

This was all her fault. She should have checked on that water pipe the night he arrived. It took weeks, dozens of conversations to get anything repaired down here. She'd known that.

"Isabela's wonderful, and I've betrayed her," Vivian said. "I'm a thousand times worse than Julio! I can't believe I'm this horrible person! Can't you pretend this never happened and go back to courting her?"

"Then it would be me who was worse than Julio."

"You can do it. You're a man."

"Great," he snarled. "I've fallen for a crazy woman."

"She's everything you said you wanted. We discussed this. You said you could plan out your life."

"And then I met you—crazy, wonderful you."

"Last night was just sex."

"Then why are you so damn mad about it? And why do I feel the way I do about you?"

"We'll get over it."

"This conversation is getting ridiculous," he said.

"I was supposed to play fairy godmother. I was supposed to get you to like her more. I don't have a clue what to do next."

"We run away together and make love for a week in a thatched hut by the sea until we can't do it another time."

"No!"

"Then we tell Isabela the truth."

She moaned.

"Then I'll tell her, since you're so afraid of her."

"I'm not afraid. I'm—"

"You're confused," he said gently, edging closer. "And so am I."

When his hand touched her arm, she shuddered.

"No, I have to tell her myself," she said. "And since I'm going to tell her the truth, I might as well level with you."

Finally knowing what she had to do, she turned toward him, and his dear, dark, handsome face struck her like a blow. Feeling sick and empty even before she spoke, she blurted it out anyway.

"Isabela bribed me to entertain you. She said if I got you to propose, she'd take me with her when she moved to the States. That's why I came." She hesitated. "I don't know why I slept with you. But I know I'm not right for you. It was just something crazy that happened because I'm scared of rep—amphibians."

"Do you have to talk so damn much?"

"All I wanted was an airplane ticket and enough money for a fresh start."

"Really? So all that fire and light and love was just for money?"

It was a ridiculous lie. Anybody could see through it, but her stubborn streak took over, and she stuck to it. She sighed. "I guess I got carried away."

"You damn sure did. So—all you want now is a ticket home and money for a fresh start?"

She locked her eyes on his dark face and nodded.

He drew a slow breath. "Well, you were worth every penny. If Isabela doesn't come through with the ticket, I damn sure will."

When the driver of the wrecker drove into the carport, Cash and Vivian had long since quit speaking. Miguelito, wearing wet swimming trunks, ran to greet them. Concho leapt up, barking, his tail thumping excitedly.

"Why didn't you come home, Mommy? *Tía* was screaming and crying. Papacito even called the police." Miguelito smiled. "But the police were too busy to come."

"Thank goodness." As she knelt, he took her hands and held on tightly. "There was a storm, my darling. We hit a wall."

"Were you hurt?" Miguelito's troubled black eyes were huge.

She shook her head and drew him closer.

"She was with me. She was fine," Cash said.

Vivian wrapped her child in her arms and hugged him fiercely. Moments later a gate slammed, and Julio strode into the carport.

"Miguelito! There you are. You're not supposed to run off without telling Papacito, where—"

"He's with me," Vivian said.

"Vivi!" Then Julio saw Cash. "I see," he murmured, his voice thick with insolence and innuendo.

Vivian lowered her eyes. "Not in front of Miguelito."

"Isabela went crazy last night," Julio said.

Vivian said nothing.

"I was worried sick about you, too," Julio persisted.

"As you see—I'm fine."

"Julio?" Tammy yelled from the other side of the wall.

"In the carport, *querida!*" Julio responded.

"We were in an accident," Cash said matter-of-factly. "The phones were out. We got back as soon as we could. Period."

She could feel the heat of Julio's eyes burning her face. She had to get Miguelito away before Julio erupted.

Tammy ran into the carport in a minuscule black bikini, water dripping down her long, golden legs.

"Take Miguelito back to the pool," Julio said.

"Thank you," Vivian said, as Tammy took the child and led him away.

"You come here to see my sister, Mr. Cash McRay, but you stay out all night with my wife."

Cash's mouth thinned. "She divorced you, remember?"

"Isabela is my sister. Vivi is the mother of my son. Vivi's vulnerable. She's family."

Vivian winced at Julio's high-handedness.

"She's all those things…and more," Cash said.

"I don't want you using her and hurting her. You're rich and famous. You overpower her better judgment."

"Give her a little credit," Cash said.

"Stop it. I won't have you discussing me like this!"

To her surprise they obeyed her. When she was sure the conversation was over, she left them to check on Miguelito.

Miguelito beamed happily when he saw her, and she smiled too.

"Watch me dive," he said.

"Don't run—"

Of course, he forgot and ran, and she had to tell him again. A few minutes later Cash stopped by the pool. His eyes were dark and his mouth still grim as he sat down in one of the heavy teak chairs beside her.

"Can we go somewhere and talk?" he said.

Her eyes on Miguelito, she leaned forward. He ran onto the diving board and began to jump up and down before he got to the end. He was so excited he wasn't concentrating on what he was doing.

"Watch me," he screamed as he leaned over the water, arms out in front, fingers pointed.

"I had a wonderful time with you," Cash said. "No matter what kind of woman you think I want, you are special—at least to me."

So are you. Cash's face was so classically chiseled it might have been one of the Mayan gods. Her stomach tightened, and she turned, squinting against the glare.

"Please—just leave me alone. I have a little boy…a little life."

"I have no life without you."

"You got laid. You're wealthy and attractive. You can have any girl. So big deal."

"You're not watching me!" Miguelito yelled, bouncing higher than he ever had before.

"Just go," she continued. "I'll tell Isabela that I seduced you. That it wasn't your fault. I'll let you off easy."

"Do you ever listen? You're the first real thing that's happened to me in a long time," he said. "I think I'm falling in love with you."

Falling in love—

She made a soft, almost inaudible sound. Julio had used those same words so easily, and she'd fallen for them hard.

Somehow she resisted the urge to throw herself into his arms and kiss him senseless. She had to be smarter this time. She had to do what was right for all of them.

"It was a dream," she said. "And dreams can't last. Isabela's the kind of woman you should marry."

"Do you ever listen? I repeat—she's not right for me."

"Do *you* listen? I love Isabela like a sister," Vivian said.

"I know. That's how I probably love her too."

"Stop it. This is tearing me to pieces. Okay?"

He nodded. She hated the way he looked so tortured and somehow defeated.

"All right," he said.

"I have to handle her my own way."

"What about us?"

Tears filled her eyes, but she blinked so he wouldn't see them. She was sorry about what she had to say, sorrier than he could ever imagine.

"What about your offer of a ticket and money for a fresh start?"

"I know what I said, damn it. I was madder than hell." He caught a breath. "I can't give you up."

The sun beat down upon his dark hair, and her body was more conscious of him than it had ever been before. It was as if he were part of her and would always be part of her. Then she looked past him to the small dark figure who was still bouncing up and down on the board.

Miguelito had moved even farther back on the board. "Darling, no. You can't jump until you're standing on the end—No!"

Cash's head whipped around. One glance at the boy bouncing so clumsily and Cash sprang toward the pool. He dove at the exact moment Miguelito's dark head hit the edge of the board and his body tumbled into the water at an angle.

Two powerful strokes and Cash was under the board, grabbing the boy by his thin arms, pulling him up to fresh air and safety. Julio bellowed orders. In no time, Cash had Miguelito at the shallow end and was lifting him out of the water into Julio's arms.

Miguelito opened his eyes and stared at his parents vaguely.

"Is he okay?" Vivian whispered.

Julio hit him so soundly on the back, the child spit out a stream of water.

"I think he's going to be fine," Cash said as he climbed out of the pool. His clothes were soaked, and water flooded the red tiles around the pool. His wet white shirt was plastered to his muscular torso. A black lock of hair fell across his dark brow, and he kept pushing it back. He looked sexy and infinitely dear.

And he had saved Miguelito.

"Feeling okay?" he asked as he knelt and pressed Miguelito's hand.

"My head hurts."

"It probably will for a while." Cash got up slowly. "I guess I'd better go change, and comb my leonine mane."

Miguelito smiled up at him, and Vivian was suddenly so terrified of her feelings for the man towering above her that she looked down at her child, not trusting herself even to thank him. Instead of dealing with those feelings, she hugged Miguelito's wet body fiercely and kissed his cheeks over and over again.

"Cash rescued you, darling" was the best she could manage by way of thanks.

"Thank you, Cash," Miguelito called, and then he turned inquisitive black eyes to her. "Why is he going away? Why are you mad at him?"

"I'm not!"

Julio eyed her suspiciously. Grabbing a towel, he wrapped the boy in it. After that he put his arms around his ex-wife and son and held them protectively, as if they belonged to him.

"The gringo must go," he said in a low tone.

"But I like him, Papacito. He saved—"

"He does not belong here."

"Can we discuss this later?" Vivian asked, meaning when Miguelito wasn't around.

She wasn't about to tell Julio that for once she agreed with him.

* * *

Stifling an unexpected attack of nervousness, Vivian straightened her shoulders and knocked softly on Isabela's carved, bedroom door. When there was no answer, she turned the handle and stepped tentatively over the threshold. The bedroom was dark because the shutters were closed, and Isabela had the lights off.

"Don't turn on the light, Vivi." Isabela's whisper floated from the bed across the shadowy vastness.

"Why didn't you answer me?"

"I was too afraid."

Guilt lodged like a fist in Vivian's throat as she headed toward the huge dark shape that was Isabela's double bed.

"How did you do as my fairy godmother?" Isabela asked in a soft, unnatural voice.

"I told you not to make me go," Vivian replied, staring dully at the floor.

"What did you two do?"

"We went to the beach house. He worked. He drew."

"That sounds so…dull." Isabela's voice was stiff.

Vivian's stomach felt queasy.

"I wish I could have been there, but—" Isabela snapped at the chain on her bedside lamp. Her face was still red and swollen, but her intense black eyes held infinite trust as she stared at Vivian. "Thank you for taking him. The doctor says I'm a little allergic after all. I can't let Cash see me like this. You have to entertain him again today."

"No!"

"Just one more day. Please—"

Dios. "There's something I have to tell you."

"I don't care about my SUV."

"That's not it. Oh, Isabela, I'm so ashamed. I love you so much."

"You slept with him?" Isabela said after a tense silence, her voice so low and wretched Vivian could barely hear her.

Vivian forced herself to meet the blazing hurt in her sister-in-law's eyes. "It was my fault. Totally my fault. Not his."

Isabela went white. "H-how could you? Never in a million years did I believe that would be your answer." Her black eyes lit up, and she grabbed her nail file and pointed it at her own heart.

Twelve

Isabela pressed the file against her chest. "If I cut out my heart, would that make you happy?"

"I'm sorry! I love you!"

"Sorry? Is that all you can say?" Isabela raised the file high.

When Vivian screamed and ran toward her, Isabela stabbed at her pillows instead of her chest. She brought the file down again and again until feathers spurted out like flurries of snow.

She plunged her file into the pillow still again. "I wish I had the courage to kill myself. I do." She lifted the torn pillowcase and waved it back and forth, sending more feathers flying.

Vivian's mouth went dry. "I feel like such a louse."

Isabela shredded the pillowcase, releasing the last of the feathers. "I was so worried and scared when you two didn't come home last night. I tried to call you—dozens and dozens of times."

"I know."

Drifting feathers settled in Isabela's black hair. One landed on the tip of her nose, and she sneezed and fanned it away. "Then I'd get paranoid and imagine you and he kissing, betraying me...but I'd tell myself those were crazy thoughts because I've got too much hot, Latin blood. One minute I was furious, the next I was terrified. I didn't sleep a wink."

"I'm sorry."

"Quit saying that. Do you think I want your pity? You were both probably laughing at me."

"No," Vivian said tenderly.

Isabela flung the nail file across the room and grabbed another pillow, hugging it to her breast. "I can't believe you're actually telling me all this—"

"You deserve the truth."

"Deserve? This isn't what I deserve. I did everything for you—"

"I know. You were wonderful."

"No Mexican would ever confess to such, for fear of being stabbed or something. Why are you standing there? Watching me? Laughing at me? Why don't you go and leave me?"

"I didn't do it on purpose. It...it just happened."

"Did he ask you to marry him?"

"It was just sex. Indiscriminate sex."

"I don't believe you. He's not like that. He almost ran every time I tried to kiss him."

"I don't care about him. And he doesn't care about me. He cares about you."

"I'm not a total *idiota*." Isabela threw her hands out and flopped backward onto her bed, sending more feathers spiraling above her. "When you leave, send the maids to clean up this mess."

"I know you can never forgive me, and I don't blame you. But forgive him. Marry him.... He needs you."

Isabela sat up. "Are you crazy? Maybe if you hadn't told me, maybe I could."

"You two haven't even begun yet. It's not like he cheated on you."

"How can you even say that?"

Vivian was backing toward the door. "I'm sorry. I feel terrible. I want to make everything all right."

"Well, you can't."

"I'll never forgive myself."

"You've been wanting to go home and I wouldn't let you. Well, I want you gone now. I'll pay for your bus ticket."

"Bus?" It was hours and hours to the States by bus.

Isabela read her mind and smiled. "You can think about how sorry you are while you stare out at the Mexican countryside. We have a beautiful country, and it is quite large. The roads are bad too." She laughed a little, as if cheered by the thought.

"Miguelito will go crazy on such a long ride."

Isabela laughed again. "We'll make that a third-class bus, then. And…and that ticket is all you'll ever get from me. As far as I'm concerned, once you get on that bus, I don't care if it breaks down in the middle of the Chihuahua desert and you have a heat stroke, or…or banditos carry you off. If you do make it to the States, I don't care if you're so poor Miguelito starves or…or…"

She broke down in tears and buried her face in her sheets so Vivian couldn't watch her cry.

"Isabela, you don't mean—"

"I mean every single word" came her muffled sobs through the wadded bedding.

Vivian was slinging jeans and shorts and blouses she intended to pack for her trip home into a huge wicker laundry basket.

"You slept with him? And you wouldn't sleep with me?" Julio whispered. Maybe he was speaking softly, but he was striding about her bedroom like an angry bear.

Furious, Vivian slung a red bra and a black silk pair of thong panties past his nose toward her basket.

"A normal woman would pack in suitcases," Julio said in husbandly disgust as he lifted the red bra off the floor. "When did you start wearing indecent underwear." He peered at her through the sheer bra.

"The way I pack is none of your business. Just as who I sleep with. And this—" she lunged and grabbed the bra "—is none of your business."

"Because of another man, you're taking my son to a violent, barbarous country—"

"The United States of America. The land of opportunity."

Cash knocked on the door and Vivian and Julio yelled in unison, "Go away!"

"It's only me." Cash pushed the door open. "And since I'm the subject of your conversation—"

She sighed, shrugging.

Julio raised a fist. "She's packing. She never wants to see you again."

"Julio, I really can do this without you."

"He slept with you, and he treats you like a dog!" Julio said to Vivian.

"You've got your nerve," Cash said.

"She's my wife!"

"Ex-wife." This time it was Cash and Vivian who spoke in unison.

When Julio lunged at Cash, Vivian jumped in front of him. His raised fist, meant for Cash's jaw, collided with her slender jaw.

"Ouch!" She fell backward and both men knelt on piles of lacy underwear to help her up.

"Get ice," Cash ordered, taking charge.

"I'm fine," she said. "Or I will be, as soon as you both leave."

"I'm the husband," Julio said. "I stay."

"Julio, please—just do as he says. I really need to talk to him."

"Alone? With all these sexy underwears."

She gave him a look. "You're not my husband anymore, you know."

"It's about time you reminded him of that fact," Cash said.

"*You*—be quiet," she whispered, pressing a fingertip to her aching jaw.

Julio bowed to her alone. "If you need me, scream."

She nodded as he let himself out.

"Why did you ever marry that lunatic?" Cash demanded.

"He's cute."

"Funny. I don't get that about him." Cash made a face and then he left her to go to the bathroom. He returned swiftly with a cold wet rag, which she took and pressed against her jawline.

"Okay. What do you want? As you can see, I'm busy packing."

"You're not traveling by third-class bus all the way to the States with a six-year-old little boy."

"It's okay. I feel sane, for the first time in years. I'm taking my life back. I'm going to get a job, go to college and become a teacher. I know that sounds ordinary to someone like—"

"Don't treat me like I'm not human."

"You're rich—"

"I also care about you. I don't want to lose you."

"You never had me. I'm a big girl. This is something I have to do. I should thank you. Maybe I wouldn't ever have had the nerve to strike out on my own if it weren't for you."

"You said you didn't want Miguelito to have to pay for any more of your mistakes."

"Don't you dare act like you care more about my son than I do."

"Did it ever occur to you that maybe being so damn independent when you can ill afford to be might be your biggest mistake? I could care for you and your son if you'd let me.

What happened last night...this whole thing...you, Miguel-ito...it means a lot to me."

"You're lonely. It doesn't take a genius to see you and I are all wrong for each other. We had great sex, but how long would our attraction last? You have a big life. You're an international player. I'm...nothing."

"We're both human beings, damn it. Why doesn't that count?"

"Our worlds are too different, just like my world was too different from Julio's for me to understand all the reasons why we wouldn't work. And we didn't. You and I couldn't either."

"Sometimes our past teaches us the wrong lessons," Cash said.

"I've been hurt."

"Join the club."

"You and me?" She laughed. "This one is a no-brainer."

"Not for me." He sighed and pushed back his thick, glorious hair. "All right, then. If you're determined, just let me at least give you the money for airline tickets and your fresh start."

"You owe me nothing."

"I want to do this as a friend."

"No."

Sucking in a hard breath, Cash stared out the window. The light slanted across his carved features in such a way that she saw the exact moment when his face darkened and closed against her.

Finally, she thought, hurting in spite of herself.

He spoke again, only this time he avoided looking at her. "All right, I'm doing this for Miguelito, not you. I've got millions. Take the money—for his sake. I'll give you enough to go back to college, enough so you won't have to borrow or worry—"

"You don't care about Miguelito." In another moment she would be sobbing.

"You don't know what I care about because you're so damn sure you know everything, and so closed off to me because I'm rich, you never listen. Well, I know what it is to grow up lonely—with parents too busy for you. If you go to school and work and he's far from his father and aunt, you'll be worried all the time about money and school. You won't have time for him. He's a little boy."

"You weren't like Miguelito. You were rich. You had everything."

"Yes," he said so bitterly she almost wondered if she really did know all about him.

"I don't want your money." But her voice shook as she thought about Miguelito. Cash had hit a nerve. She would be taking her son away from everything and everybody he loved. Her future and his would be frighteningly uncertain. She'd have Miguelito to think about and care about. Money could ease a lot of stress. She'd be able to be gentler and more patient with him.

"Suit yourself," Cash said. Then he turned his back on her and headed out the door. His strides were long, determined, as if he were now as anxious to get away from her as she'd told him she was to be free of him.

She couldn't stop thinking about what he'd said about his lonely childhood, about how she might make Miguelito suffer more than he already had with the divorce.

"Cash—" Her voice was drowned out when he slammed the door.

Swallowing her pride, she ran after him into the hallway. "Cash! Wait, please…"

This time he turned. He looked huge in the shadowy hall, but she padded up to him anyway.

"You were right," she managed to say. "I don't want anything from you, but…maybe I'm in no position to refuse."

He started to say something and then bit it back when he read the sorrow in her eyes and the pride in her tortured face.

She squared her shoulders. "So, I—I'll take your money,"

she whispered. "I'll take it—but I'll pay you back—a little every month, with interest."

"Damn it. I don't care about you paying me back—"

Her heart slammed, slowly, painfully. "But maybe I do. Maybe I don't want to owe you or anybody else anything ever again."

He swallowed a quick violent breath. "Damn your pride…and your guilt. Both are misplaced. Is it so wrong for me to want to take care of you because I can? Would it be so awful to try to love me?"

Love. She loved him. But love didn't last. At least not for her. Love always went away.

She stared at her bare feet, too miserable for words. It wouldn't work, and when it didn't, the pain for both of them would be unbearable.

She felt his warm hand lift her chin. "I've made you unhappy," he said in a gentle voice. "That's the last thing I ever want to do."

"I'll be okay," she said weakly, unable to say more because she was afraid she might break and then he'd see through her little act.

"Hell, I'll write the check. Then I'll go, if that's what you want. My address will be on my check. Not that I expect anything from you ever." He paused. "And for what it's worth, it was nice knowing you—Aphrodite. Damn nice. Whether you believe it or not, I'll never forget you."

"Just go," she said softly, closing her eyes, fighting tears harder than ever because she feared he'd take her in his arms and she'd never have the strength to leave him.

When she opened her eyes again, he was gone, and Miguelito was there, slipping his hand into hers.

"Cash said I won't ever see him again. Why not, Mommy? I asked him if he's mad at you, and he said he loves you. Do you hate him too? Like you used to hate Daddy…after the divorce?"

She knelt and fingered his collarless T-shirt. Never as long as she lived would she feel free of guilt for divorcing Julio and separating Miguelito from his father. But there wasn't anything she could do about it but live with it. Miguelito would have to live with it too. She only hoped it would make him stronger.

"Darling, I don't hate your father or Cash, but you have to pack. We're going home."

"This is my home."

"Not anymore."

"Can we take Spot with us?"

"His name is Concho. And I'm not sure we can manage a dog."

"*Tía* doesn't want him." Miguelito wiped at his eyes.

"She doesn't want *us* either," Vivian murmured under her breath and continued packing.

Thirteen

──

Four months later
San Francisco, California

The clock on the landing struck midnight as Cash slammed the front door. Claws clicked on parquet flooring. Spot ran up barking.

"Shh." Cash scratched the orange woolly head when the beast rushed him, his tail thumping wildly.

Cash felt drained from jet lag and the gala fund-raiser he'd finally managed to escape. Roger, however, was full of energy and determined to have one more for the road. The younger man raced ahead of him down the hall to the elaborate bar Cash kept in his dining room.

Impatient for his assistant to be gone, Cash unknotted his tie. From his bar came the sounds of the bar refrigerator door opening and closing, of ice clinking into a crystal glass, of a scotch bottle being opened—no doubt his good fifty-year-old stuff.

"Hey—this is great. Can I fix you something?" Roger called jovially.

"No thanks." Cash yanked his tie through his collar and tossed it carelessly onto a French burlwood table. He shrugged out of his jacket and slung it onto the worn Aubusson carpet that had once graced the entrance of his grandmother's grand house in Martha's Vineyard.

Smiling, Roger emerged from the hall, drink in hand. "I couldn't believe how much you let our beautiful hostess clip you for tonight."

Cash frowned. "I was tired I guess."

"You couldn't tell it. You talked to everybody."

Cash sighed. "Yes, I talked too much, laughed too much and damn sure drank too much." He'd done all those things to excess lately to extinguish every thought and feeling he had about a certain unforgettable woman. "I have a helluva headache as a result."

"When did you get in from Paris?"

"Yesterday. I got to the office before dawn."

"The place sure was backed up." Roger sipped, watching him. "So, tell me about Europe. The papers made it sound like you partied nonstop with those aristocratic friends whose estate you were redoing. Another one of Count Leopoldo's pads, right?"

Cash was stroking Spot behind the ears now, and the dog wore an expression of appreciative bliss. "You met him in Florence."

"Oh, right. Every magazine that counts said your designs for his palace in the Alps were brilliant and his parties and cruises were A-list. Did you have any fun?"

"I missed Spot."

Roger laughed. "The mutt doesn't have a spot on him."

"He's a plain dog. He needs a plain name."

Cash sighed. *Hell, he'd missed her. Most of all he'd missed her.* A scowl worked between his brows. "I thought you read all about what I did in Europe."

"I read beautiful babes threw themselves at you."

"What if I told you that was the most grueling part?"

Roger flashed his wide smile. "Damn. What I wouldn't give to change places with you. Except you can keep Spot."

"So, you wouldn't believe me if I told you the parties and the women weren't any fun, that it's tough being chased when you don't want to be caught—even if the predators are gorgeous."

"I need another drink to swallow that one."

"Sometimes I'm not sure I can afford you."

"You can. I do your books—remember?"

Remembering all the women, Cash leaned against a fluted column in utter exhaustion. Each woman had been younger and more energetic than the one before. Ever since Mexico, ever since *her*, he'd been afraid to stop running.

Roger returned with his drink, and stared at his boss and the orange dog looking up at him with dreamy brown eyes.

"My life feels like a merry-go-round of work, absurd social obligations and women," Cash said.

"Poor little rich guy. What happened in Mexico? You went to that barbaric land to get a woman and you brought home that ugly mutt—"

Spot looked at Roger and moaned.

"Isabela was a mistake."

"Before you went, you told me that any woman from your same class with the proper credentials would do."

"I was a damn fool." Passion for a woman who didn't want him gave Cash's tone an abraded edge.

Roger squinted at him over the top of his glass. "You met someone else?"

"I don't want to talk about her…er…it." When he stopped petting Spot, the animal whined and licked his fingers.

"You let her go. Someone—inappropriate?"

"I said I don't—"

"You're still in love with her!" Roger observed.

"Finish your drink and get the hell out of here."

"Aren't you going to do something about her?"

"Roger!" Cash rubbed his temples. "I have a raging headache. It's late, and I'm tired." Cash went to the door and opened it.

Spot barked joyously and bounded outside. He ran up the hill and disappeared.

"Oh god. *You* were supposed to run—not him!"

"Will he come back?"

"More likely a few neighbors will show up complaining about his crimes first. He likes to turn trash cans over and send them rolling down the hills. Just go."

Roger set his glass down on the burlwood table, shot him a wry smile, and walked out. But as soon as he was gone, Cash wished him back because without Spot or him, the house felt unbearably hollow.

Vivian didn't want him. How long would it take, how many women would it take, before he could forget her?

Eventually Spot would come back and bark when he wanted in, so it was no use going after him. Grabbing his tie and jacket, Cash slung them over his shoulder and headed up the staircase toward his bedroom. His five-story house had magnificent views of the Bay Bridge and Oakland. He'd bought the place for the views. Not that he cared about them now.

The phone rang, and his idiotic heart leaped at the memory of a naked redhead reflected in seven mirrors. Maybe... He raced up the stairs into his bedroom and lunged across his bed, knocking the phone to the floor as he grabbed the receiver.

"Has she called you yet?" whispered a surly, heavily accented male voice that sounded unpleasantly familiar despite a lousy connection.

"Who is this? Where are you?"

"Julio."

A vise clamped around Cash's chest.

"Vivian's husband."

"Ex-husband."

"I told her to call you. Did she?"

"You sound drunk."

Julio laughed bitterly. "So what if I am? *Soy em-bo-ra-chado.* So what?"

Cash rubbed his brow. "It's late."

"Just call her, *bastardo.*"

"Is she in some kind of—"

Julio spit out her phone number. Not that Cash needed it. He'd called Isabela and endured an awkward conversation weeks earlier to get it.

The line went dead.

Cash told himself to ignore Julio's drunken gibes, but his caller ID revealed an unidentified caller had called him ten times today, and Julio's had come in as that of an unidentified caller.

Cash was in a panic as he dialed Vivian. Not that she answered. At this hour surely she was there. Like the other times when he'd called, her machine picked up, and he was forced to leave a message.

The French Quarter
New Orleans, Louisiana

Vivian was lying awake in the dark watching the oak branch scratch at the window and counting cracks in her ceiling. A friend of her uncle's had found her this charming one-bedroom apartment in a French colonial, one-story cottage. Not that it felt like home yet.

But it would. She just had to give it time. The windows reached the ground, and its front door opened directly onto a noisy sidewalk. A loud jazz band was playing at the corner bar. Revelers shouted at each other in the street. Not that the music was bothering her. She had much too much on her mind.

When the ringing of the phone shattered the early morning

stillness of her bedroom, Vivian sprang up and jammed a pillow over it, so it wouldn't wake Miguelito.

"Julio—I told you not to keep calling me—" When it rang again and she could still hear it, she stuffed another pillow on top of the other one.

Julio was driving her crazy with his calls at all hours. Somehow she had to make him understand he had no right to make her decisions. Finally, on the fourth ring her machine picked up.

When Cash's voice came on instead, she shuddered. Before she thought, she'd reached for the phone. Just touching the cool plastic receiver while he talked sent a tremor through her and made her feel connected to him.

She no longer noticed the trailing branch of the oak tree scratching the window or heard the strains of the jazz band. All she could do was strain to listen to Cash's huskily drawling voice.

When he finally slammed the phone down, she picked up the receiver and cradled it to her chest. Then she played his message again.

"Vivian? If you're there… Oh, hell… Julio said I should call."

Julio—

"I know you're there. Pick up. Is there something I should know? Is something wrong? You don't need to send me those damn checks, you know. I'm worried about you. Call me."

She pressed her fingertips against her mouth.

"Please call. I'm worried about you…and Miguelito."

There was a long silence. Then he left several phone numbers before hanging up.

Wondering what to do, she wadded up her pillow and buried her face in it. It seemed hours before dawn.

The morning was a soft gray and smelled of rain. As soon as Miguelito went out into the courtyard to play underneath the oak trees dripping with Spanish moss, Vivian called Julio.

"Did *he* call you?" Julio demanded.

"Yes. I didn't answer."

Julio cursed vividly.

"You shouldn't have called him," she said. "I don't need a man to rescue me!"

"You're scared and pregnant."

As if she didn't know.

She drew a deep breath. Okay, so she was scared. "I can do this, Julio. Smart, independent women aren't controlled by what they do in bed."

"Then be run by this. If you don't tell Cash about the baby, I'll find a way to take Miguelito back to Mexico."

Vivian caught her breath. "Just because I walked down the aisle with you, doesn't mean you can run my life forever."

"Not forever, *querida.* Until you marry again and have a husband to take care of you and Miguelito…and the baby."

"Women don't need men."

"You damn sure got pregnant, didn't you? Twice. You didn't do that without a man."

She lapsed into silence, pondering the mysteries of the body. The female body was powerful. It led a woman places that she wasn't sure she belonged. Why did she always have to suffer life-changing consequences for her impulsive behavior? Why could other people get away with things while her life had to take these crazy, unexpected turns? Cash had used a condom. He hadn't wanted a baby.

"Isabela shouldn't have told you, Julio. You had no right to call Cash. Why did you do that? You don't even like him."

"You've got two days before I call him back and spell it out! Now, put Miguelito on the phone—"

"Don't you dare call Cash back."

"Just get Miguelito. I don't want to talk to a crazy woman."

"When you two are done, I want to talk to Isabela."

"Claro, mi amor," he said huskily, blowing her a kiss.

When she gave Miguelito the phone, he said only a few words before ducking his head shyly and running out into the courtyard, where he crouched behind the thick trunk of an oak and spoke to his father in a secretive, whispery voice. Watching him from the window, she grew edgier by the minute.

What was Julio telling the boy? Finally, he darted back inside, stared at her belly with big scared eyes and mumbled that *Tía* wanted to talk to her.

"What did your father tell you?"

"*Nada. Tía* wants to talk to you. Can I go?"

Though furious at Julio, Vivian smiled at her son. Her hands shook when she nodded and took the receiver.

"Isabela! For this, I forgave you for sending me and Miguelito away? For this I welcomed you into my little apartment when you stood at my door holding all those roses and weeping and begging my forgiveness? Guess what your brother did? He called Cash, and I think he just told Miguelito."

"No, I forgave *you*, Vivi. I flew to New Orleans and found you. But only because the minute you left, the servants sulked so much that living in my own house was a new kind of hell."

"You promised you weren't going to tell Julio."

"It was an accident, *querida*...like your pregnancy. He gave me wine. He is my little brother. He tricked me, okay?"

"Not okay. He called Cash."

"But, Vivi, Julio has a point. Cash is the father of your baby. We are all family."

"Cash and I were only together one night."

"So? You got pregnant. Leaving him was your decision, not his. I think he loves you."

"I had my reasons."

"Crazy *gringa* reasons."

"This isn't Mexico. I want my own identity...an education. Up here women are people too."

"Down here women are women and men are men. You *gringas* are too stubborn for your own good. You want to be independent when one of the most fantastic men you've ever met wants you?"

"He's too fantastic. I don't deserve him."

"That is stupid. Down here, women tell the fathers of their children they are expecting."

"If he had a choice, he would never marry a woman like me."

"Why did you steal him from me...and then throw him away?"

"Look, I read about him in the major gossip magazines. I've seen dozens of shots of him at openings and galas with beautiful women on his arm, each girl lovelier and younger than the last."

"See, you're jealous. Because you love him."

"I don't want to drag him down, when one of those other women could make him happy.

"Don't be such a little fool. Call him. Let him decide."

"Trust me on this. It's better this way."

"What idiot is it better for? You? The baby? Miguelito? Cash?"

For moments the air was charged. Then Isabela said, "I'm dating someone you know. An American. Aaron. You were teaching him Spanish. He came by looking for you. We started talking and we couldn't stop. He's too old, but we've been having lots of fun together. He's teaching me how to sail."

"Isabela, I miss you. I miss you so much."

"You can come home anytime you want, you know."

When they hung up, Vivian felt very very alone.

Dear Isabela. Even though Vivian had stolen Cash from her, she'd surprised Vivian by how quickly she'd put Vivian's and Miguelito's welfare before her own. Vivian's plane had hardly landed in the Big Easy before Isabela flew up to Louisiana and begged her forgiveness. Once Vivian had let her inside her apartment, they'd both collapsed in each other's arms in tears and laughter.

Then Isabela, who'd seen how bare her tiny apartment was, had taken her shopping and been more generous than ever before. She'd bought new clothes for Miguelito and darling knickknacks for the apartment.

Maybe with time, Vivian would accept her condition, would get on her feet and turn the apartment into a real home. Maybe with time, she'd become independent. But first she had to find a way to remove Cash McRay from her heart and mind.

No way could she call him and tell him about the baby.

Fourteen

———

San Francisco

Cash was sprawled behind his mammoth desk in his airy office with its dazzling views of the bay. He was feeling nuts after a long day. Not that he wanted to go home or to any of the parties penciled under today's date on his calendar.

One minute, Cash was idly sifting through his personal mail and listening to Roger flirt with Leah, Cash's secretary, beyond his open door. The next, his hand shook when he slid a long, pale blue envelope from the bottom of his mail. His eyes narrowed on the return address of the classy antique shop in the French Quarter printed in precise, small letters.

Vivian worked at the shop. He'd learned this from Marco, whom Isabela kept informed. Thank God Isabela's jealousy was like a hot fire that burned like unholy hell but went out quickly. She'd called him. They'd had a friendly chat about a party they were both going to. But mostly they'd talked about Vivian.

It was the first of the month, so Cash should have been expecting Vivian's check. She hadn't returned his calls. As a result Cash had been hell on wheels for the last few days. His staff, even the usually unfazable Roger, had taken to walking out of rooms when he entered.

Not that Cash blamed them. He didn't like himself much either most of the time these days. The trouble with a bad mood was how everybody bounced it back in your face.

Cash slashed the envelope open, hoping for a note, but as always, a single green slip of paper, her check—for one hundred dollars—fluttered onto his desk. He grabbed it and wadded it up, only to look up and see Leah and Roger standing together in the doorway, watching him.

Carefully, Cash unwadded the check.

"That bad, huh?" Leah said.

He waved the crumpled check at them. "Deposit this before it bounces," he growled. "The woman who wrote it is not to be trusted."

"You must have met her in Mexico," Roger said.

"I like her already," Leah added.

Leah was in her forties and had lots of self-confidence. She was tall and long-waisted, with short wiry brown curls. She could be beautiful or not, depending on her clothes or her mood or her hairdo. She was smart and efficient, and when she smiled and meant it, she could brighten a man's worst day.

Today she wore a stretchy black sheath. She looked so good Roger couldn't stop looking at her.

She picked up the check and purred the last name, rolling the final *r* in an infuriating way. "Escobar-r-r-r? Any kin to Isabela and Marco Escobar-r-r-r?"

Roger's permanent smile was way too bright. "Escobar," he repeated, pronouncing it correctly.

Leah lifted her thick, penciled auburn brows when Cash didn't look up. "Does she have anything to do with what's been eating you lately?"

Bingo.

"You're supposed to be my secretary, not my therapist," Cash snapped.

"You don't have a therapist, so I'm pinch-hitting."

"Well, stop it, Leah."

"You should take a day off," Roger said.

"You're driving all of us crazy," Leah began. "Ever since Mexico, when you visited the Escobar-r-r-rs. Which reminds me, Isabela Escobar-r-r called while you were at lunch."

"The plot thickens," Roger said, grinning.

"The r-trilling is getting on my nerves," Cash growled.

"I'm taking Spanish in night school," Leah said. "Just practicing, sir."

Roger laughed. Cash didn't.

"Well, your Miss Escobar-r, oops, well, she said her plane landed safely, and she and her father would meet you at the gala tonight for the opening of the hospital wing you designed."

"Wilhelm Meredith also called about the Berlin project," Roger began.

The huge project his firm had bid on for Meredith had been rejected last week. "I've got his number." Cash's voice was grim.

"Maybe when you see Isabel Escobar-r—"

Cash glared, and she quit trilling instantly. Roger had to cover his mouth to keep from laughing.

"Out! Both of you!" When neither of them budged, Cash got up and slammed the door. Then he began to pace.

His love life was the problem and he knew it. Knowing that didn't make him any happier with them or himself. They shouldn't joke or tease. This wasn't funny.

He was behaving like a fool. He needed to move on. But how?

He'd called Vivian after the first check arrived. She'd hung up on him. He'd called her the next month. She'd hung up on him. The next time he'd called, she'd had an answering machine—and it had been on ever since. Ever since Julio's call, he hadn't been able to concentrate on anything. His designs were off. Hell, his whole damn life felt off.

He broke his pencil and pitched it into the trash. Then he opened his door and stormed out past Leah and Roger, knocking a trash can into the blinds. The can rolled, banging against a long window beside her desk.

"Have a nice evening," she called after him cheerily.

Cash was too afraid of Roger's big, annoying grin to turn around.

When he reached the exit, it was all he could do to resist slamming the door closed behind him.

It was a beautiful night, clear and cool. The hospital wing was beautifully landscaped, with a long bar set up near some high hedges. Tables and chairs were scattered beneath small blue and white party tents. Hundreds of people were clustered together, talking loudly.

Isabela was beautiful in black silk and gold jewelry. She stood out like the brightest jewel in a sumptuous crown, even in that dazzling crowd. Even though she was at the bar surrounded by at least a dozen admiring men, she beamed when she saw him. He went up to her, and she kissed him.

"You look wonderful," he murmured, inhaling her perfume.

"You look like you're working too hard," she replied. "You have terrible circles under your eyes."

He frowned.

"You've lost weight," she continued. "You look positively gaunt."

"Have you seen *her* lately?" Cash asked, leading her away from the others.

"Oh, yes. As I told you, we made up almost immediately. Imagine—she stole you from me, and my servants took her side. She called them on the phone all the time. They told me

Miguelito was crying for Julio and me every night. I couldn't stand it.''

"Neither the hell can I," he said woodenly.

"I couldn't lose you and her and Miguelito. So, one day I just went out to the airport and got on the first plane to New Orleans. The ticket cost a fortune. What can I say? I guess I realized I was marrying you because of who you were, and you were doing the same thing. She honestly fell in love with you. She's stubborn and opinionated, but she's very honest.''

"She said it was just sex.''

"She's a crazy *gringa*. After Julio, she's running scared. She thinks you're way up on some pedestal and she's just a little secretary in an antique shop going to night school.''

"I don't know if I believe you.''

"You should see her apartment. Awful. Tiny. Soulless. But I guess it's all she can afford.''

"She sends me a hundred dollars a month.''

"She can't afford to, and she's too proud to take a dime from me now. She says I supported her too long. I told her, she repaid me a hundredfold by running the house and the servants. Besides, she's family.''

"I call her, but she won't take my calls.''

"Back to that first visit. I took Maria with me because I was afraid to face her alone. When we got there, Maria rang the doorbell. Miguelito opened the door and ran into my arms while Vivian stood behind him just inside the apartment. Finally, I dared to look up at her. She has the softest eyes when they're full of tears…like crushed blue violets.''

"I know that look. She forgave you, then?''

"In a heartbeat. We hugged and cried and then we laughed that we'd behaved like such idiots.''

"Did you talk about me?''

"I'm not that crazy.''

He felt hurt and left out, so he hardened his jaw in an attempt not to show it.

"But she loves you, you big *idioto*," Isabela said. "And she loves me."

"How can you be so sure—I mean about me?"

"How can you both be crazy? She would never sleep with a man she didn't love."

"But I'd only known her one day."

"So? Don't you believe in magic? In love at first sight?"

"Hell, no."

"Not even when it's happened to you?"

He stared at her.

"*Gringo. Estùpido.* You two belong together."

"I miss the hell out of her. I dream about Botticelli a lot," he said. "Vivian's always stepping out of the paintings wearing nothing. Only then I wake up, and she vanishes."

"You love her?"

"I think about her all the time. I want to tell her about my day, ask her stupid questions. But—love at first sight? That's a stretch."

"For a genius, you're not too bright. And another thing— if you don't go see her immediately, Julio is going to turn up on your doorstep."

"Why?"

"*Hola.* Hello. One plus one sometimes equals more than two."

"She's not…"

"Pregnant." Isabela raised her brows and began to nod at him. When he froze, she smiled. "You've made me a *tía* again."

"Oh God." He bolted for the exit.

At the sound of his dropped glass breaking, heads turned, and Isabela doubled over with laughter.

Vivian was on the phone in the cramped back office of the luxurious antique shop where she worked in the Quarter, when the deliveryman arrived with two large vases of white lilies decorated with Mexican rattles and red and blue ribbons.

"But the porcelains didn't arrive, and we have to have them," Vivian was saying.

"Where do you want the rest of the flowers?" the deliveryman asked.

"The rest?"

"Our van is full, and they're all for you."

"What?"

"You've got a wealthy admirer, *chère*."

"I'll have to call you back," she said into the mouthpiece.

Thirty minutes later the deliveryman had his van unloaded. The antique shop brimmed with exotic Mexican blossoms. Vivian went from bouquet to bouquet of lilies and hibiscus blossoms and inhaled the sweet fragrance of the lilies as she read the cards. The flowers were from Cash, and every card said "I love you."

A second truck pulled up with still more flowers, and they were all for her too. When she stepped outside to direct the deliverymen, she gasped in wonder. A tall man with gorgeous black hair and a broad chest was striding toward her. He looked sleek and powerful, even in his elegantly cut gray suit, and even though he was smiling at her uncertainly.

"Cash—" Her voice cracked. Then she backed into the brick wall and froze. "W-why aren't you in San Francisco where you belong?"

"Because you aren't there." Then he touched her bare arm with the back of his knuckles, and her body shook all over with want and need and anguish.

"Because I missed you," he said in that velvet tone that undid her.

She caught the smell of his starched cotton shirt as well as the scent of his skin and cologne, and sighed. "I know what you mean."

"You didn't call."

"You shouldn't have sent all the flowers. They're way too expensive."

"I can afford them. I'm rich remember?"

She was thrilled he was here, but her pleasure was laced with the terrible tension that stretched between them. "You should have just called or something."

"You don't answer your phone."

"Well, you shouldn't have come all this way."

"Don't you have something important to tell me?" he asked.

Her gaze darted fearfully to his face. "Did Julio or Isabela tell you, because if they—"

"What does it matter? I'm here, willing to start where we left off…if you are."

"Cash…"

"Can we go somewhere? A café or something?"

"I—I'll ask my boss."

A few minutes later, she led him to the café around the corner. He ordered them black coffee and beignets as if they were an ordinary couple.

"Just my luck," she said after she told him about the baby. "We go to bed once and I get pregnant. I know you couldn't possibly want…and I don't expect—"

He pulled a velvet box out of his pocket and pushed it across the red-checkered tablecloth toward her. "For what it's worth, I do want." His gaze locked on her face. "I'm asking you to marry me, Vivian."

She stroked the soft velvet but didn't open the box. "I thought you'd be furious because I didn't tell you."

His knuckles went white. He was very still. "I'm not saying we don't have a lot of things to work on in our relationship."

His face was cast in bitter lines. If he were anyone other than who he was, she might have believed she'd hurt him deeply. But he was big and important, and she'd seen pictures of him with famous beauties.

"But I'm willing to try," he finished.

She told herself she'd hurt his pride, not him. "It wouldn't work…for so many reasons."

"It won't if you don't give us a chance. It is surprising what challenges can be conquered if you decide to face them head-on."

"Is that really all it takes?" she asked hesitantly.

"Sometimes."

"You're famous."

"You will be too—if you marry me."

"That's not funny. Everybody will be counting the months."

"I don't care. Do you?"

"This isn't some fairy tale. We knew each other a couple of days. Guys like you pay doctors to take care of problems like this when you get girls like me pregnant."

He was silent for a long time, silent until the air seemed so charged with the heavy weight of some unspoken, tortured emotion, she hardly dared to breathe.

"I'm not that guy—no matter how your fears and self-doubts keep inventing him. I want to be part of this baby's life. Part of your life. But if you don't want to marry me, we'll do this your way. I'll help you any way you want, anytime. I won't pressure you. But for what it's worth—I love you. And I want to spend the rest of my life loving you. Life isn't about being famous, you know. It's about family. I've always wanted a real family."

She couldn't believe he was voicing her own dream. Too miserable for words or hope, she shook her head.

He got up slowly, and she fought back tears.

Then he said, "Tell Miguelito I'm sorry I missed him. It would have been nice hanging out with him for a lifetime. He's a cute kid. A real heartbreaker. Like his mother. Like my little Sophie. If you decided to marry me, I would have to put in a swimming pool." He paused, waiting. Finally, he sighed. "Goodbye, Vivian."

She tried to speak, but her throat clenched too tightly.

"Well, at least I tried," he said, picking up the ring and placing it in his pocket.

Then he was outside the door—gone. And she could do nothing but sit there and wipe her damp lashes with her paper napkin. Finally, she closed her eyes and covered her face with her hands. It was her body, her pregnant, hormone-besieged body that was making her so crazy, making her feel so desperately lost and alone that she almost believed he was right…that life really was about the little moments…that like her he needed to be part of a real family…that they could make it work.

It's surprising what challenges can be conquered if you decide to face them head-on.

Was he right? What if he was?

The thought of going back to her bleak apartment, of facing years alone without him finally got the best of her.

Hardly knowing what she was doing, she stood up and stumbled out of the café into the soft, gray light. Then she saw him and began running down the sidewalk, pushing through people who got in her way, calling his name.

"Cash! Cash—"

When he turned, his chiseled face looked lost and haunted—until she smiled at him. Then his expression lit up, and his lips parted into a grin that filled her entire being with hope and happiness. Suddenly he was cutting through the crowd toward her. She was in his arms, and he was lifting her and twirling her round and round, so that other pedestrians stopped to watch them and smile.

Never removing his gaze from her face, he eased her back to the ground slowly as if she were very precious to him and pulled the ring box from his pocket.

"I—I don't know about this," she whispered, opening the velvet box and peeping at the big diamond that winked at her. "It's too huge for a girl like me."

"It's flawless." He took the ring out and slid it onto her finger. "But if you don't like it, you can pick out one you do. We'll take it one day at a time."

She shook her head. "Marrying you is the easy way out."

"Who says marriage is easy? Any marriage? Your first one wasn't. Half of them don't work out. Being rich isn't what it's cracked up to be either. And you haven't tried to live with me. I get into hellish artistic funks. When I'm working, I hole up for weeks and ignore everybody."

"I guess your wife would have to learn to be her own person."

"You can be anything you want to be if you let yourself believe in possibilities. I love you. Please don't send me away." He lowered his mouth until it was very close to hers.

"Kiss me," she whispered. "Make me believe. I'm in the mood for a miracle."

His hands cupped her face gently, reverently, and he stared into her eyes for a long time and smiled.

He loved her. She could see it so plainly.

His kiss was soft at first and then harder, slowly growing hotter. All too soon, her body took over.

"You're not going back to work today," he said, his breathing rough and irregular now. "We're going to my hotel."

For once she didn't argue other than to say, "We have an hour and a half before I have to pick up Miguelito."

"I can't wait to see him," Cash said.

Then he kissed her again, and every cell in her being ached for what was to come. His hard mouth was both tender and passionate, and she felt warm tears of joy sting her eyelids.

"I love you," she said, wrapping her arms around his big body. "I missed you."

"You damn sure made me miserable for a while."

"I was miserable too. Does that count?"

"Yeah. It counts. But you have a lot to make up for," he said.

"We have the rest of our lives."

"You can start during the next hour and a half. I have a long list...."

"What exactly do you have in mind?"

When he leaned down and whispered into her ear, she grew so hot, she knew her face must be scarlet. He hugged her close, and they kissed again.

The moon was bright, the dark Pacific splashed with silver. Cash was lying in bed in the most fantastic bedroom in the most fantastic house she'd ever seen. Behind the bed was an eight-paneled painting with eight naked Aphrodites rising out of the sea.

The mansion with its flying decks clung to a cliff over Acapulco. Not that she was that interested in the magnificent house when Cash's dark, muscular body was sprawled across the white satin sheets.

"Marco and I designed it for a friend," Cash said lazily, watching her as she padded about the thick white carpet brushing her red hair out.

"I'm so glad he loaned it to us."

"It was a wedding gift, my love," Cash said.

"And this is our wedding night," she whispered.

"So—strip," he murmured, "or do I have to get up and do it for you?"

She leaned down to turn out the light.

"Leave it on."

Shyly she lowered the strap of her filmy, apricot-colored negligee over her slim arm and winked at him.

"Take your time," he said.

She whirled round and round, causing the gauzy gown to flow around her, revealing her legs and thighs and the thatch of red curls between her legs. Then she grabbed the hem of her skirt, pulled it over her head and tossed it at him.

"That was fast. I said slowly."

"You know me better than that."

"And just like I remembered…you're better than Botticelli."

"I'm so glad you think so. If only we had a big shell, we

could go down to the ocean and I could step out of it," she laughed.

"You'd give every Mexican in Acapulco a heart attack."

He got out of bed and took her in his arms. "I've been dreaming about you stepping out of paintings naked. Only I wake up and you vanish."

"I'll be here when you wake up."

He lowered his mouth to hers, and soon nothing mattered to Cash but the wonderful feel of her warm body touching and cavorting with his. She felt silky, fluid, alive and on fire. Her heart beat like a drum.

"Get in bed," he said huskily.

But he stood there, holding her and kissing her until she was breathless.

"I can't go anywhere if you don't stop kissing me."

"And I can't stop kissing you, so there."

"They'll find us like this…petrified and still kissing," she teased.

"I don't think so."

When they finally made it to the bed, he took his time, nibbling her with his mouth and licking her with his tongue until every cell felt like it was pulsing and she had never felt so burstingly alive.

The instant he thrust inside her, they came together, shuddering, clinging, moaning as their bodies clenched in spasms. After a short rest, he made love to her again. And then again.

"Tomorrow we're flying to Florence for the rest of our honeymoon," he murmured afterward, stroking her hair. "There's a painting I want to show you."

"I think I know which one."

"The last time I saw it, I thought I could plan my life."

"Then you met me. And my life never goes according to plan."

"I couldn't have planned anything better. You're the perfect bride for me…even if you took a little taming."

"You want to know why?" she asked.

"Why?"

"Because nobody in the whole world is ever going to love you the way I will."

"I know," he agreed. "And nobody is ever going to love you the way I will either."

She smiled radiantly.

"I was wondering what it would take to convince you," he said.

"Good thing you're a patient man."

"That's a virtue I never knew I had." He smiled.

"Until you met me."

"I don't think my staff in San Francisco would agree."

She laughed and pulled him close. "I want to do it again."

"I don't think I can."

But her mouth moved down his body and kissed him until he was hard again, and she climbed on top.

Afterward, when they lay wrapped in each other's arms in the dark lit only by stars, she said, "See, you were right."

"About what?"

"You said it's surprising what challenges can be conquered if you decide to face them head-on."

"I was inspired. I had you."

"Always. Forever," she promised.

* * * * *

We hope you enjoyed
THE BRIDE TAMER.

In Ann Major's next story, sexy, revenge-
hungry Cole Knight has met his match in
THE GIRL WITH THE GOLDEN SPURS,
coming in October 2004
from MIRA Books.

For a sneak preview of
THE GIRL WITH THE GOLDEN SPURS,
turn the page...

Prologue

The devil had dealt from the bottom of the deck one time too many.

An eye for an eye, the Bible said. Or at least Cole Knight had heard somewhere the good book said something like that. To tell the truth, he wasn't much of a biblical scholar. But he loved God, the hot, thorny land under his boots that by all rights should have been his, and his family—in that order. He was willing to die for them, too.

Maybe that was overstating the case. To tell the truth, Cole Knight wasn't much of anything. Wasn't likely to be either. Not if Caesar Kemble and his bunch had their way.

But where was it written you couldn't kill a man on the same day you buried your good for nothin' father and set things right? Especially if the man was the cause of your old man's ruin? And yours, too?

Hell, it was about time somebody stood up and demanded justice. The Knights had as much right, more right, as the Kembles to be here.

Cole Knight belonged here. Trouble was, he didn't own a single acre. The Kembles had stripped him to the bone.

The feud between the Kembles and the Knights went back more than a hundred years. It had all begun when the first Caesar Kemble, the original founder of the Golden Spurs, had died without a will, and his son Johnny Kemble had cheated his adopted sister, Carolina Knight, out of her share. The Knights were direct descendants of Carolina Knight, whose

biological father had been a partner of the original Caesar
Kemble.

As if that hadn't been bad enough, four more generations
of Kembles had continued to cheat and steal even more land
from the Knights. The Knights' vast holdings, which had once
been even bigger than the Kembles', had shrunk to a miserable fifty thousand acres. Worst of all, not long ago, Cole's
father had lost those last fifty thousand acres in a card game.

Thus, the Kembles were Texas royalty. The Knights were
dirt.

Cole had already been to the barn to saddle Dr. Pepper. No
sooner had Sally McCallie, the last hypocritical mourner,
waddled out of the dilapidated ranch house than Cole was out
of his sticky, black wool suit and into his jeans and boots. A
few seconds later his long, lean body was stomping down the
backstairs into the sweltering, late July heat. Thrusting his
rifle into his worn scabbard, he seized the reins, and threw
himself onto the horse.

The rickety screen door banged shut behind him. There was
finality in that summertime sound. His daddy was dead, his
bloated face as gray and nasty under the waxy makeup as wet
ash, and Cole's own unhappy boyhood was over.

It was just as well. Hell, he was twenty-four. Not that he
had much to show for it. He'd had to quit college after his
older brother, Shanghai, who'd been putting him through
school, had unearthed some incriminating original bank doc-
uments and journals, which proved Carolina had been swin-
dled. When Shanghai had threatened to sue the Kembles, Caesar had run him off. Shanghai had left in the middle of the
night without even saying goodbye. Without Shanghai's help
and with an ailing father to support, Cole hadn't had money
to pay tuition much less the time to spend on school.

Twenty-four and broke, Cole was the last of the line and
going nowhere. At least that's what the locals thought. Like
a lot of young men, he seethed with ambition and the desire
to set things right.

Too bad he took after his old man, local folk said. Too bad his brother Shanghai, who'd shown such promise, had turned out to be as sorry as the rest of the Knights when he'd abandoned his dying father.

So much for the locals. After today, if Cole got lucky, they'd have a new morsel of gossip about him to chew on. They could choke on it for all he cared.

Cole felt almost good riding toward the immense Golden Spurs Ranch. Finally, he was doing something about the crimes of the past and present that had made his soul fester. Partly he felt better because he couldn't get on a horse without relaxing a little. Cowboying had been born in him. It was as natural to him as breathing, eating and chasing pretty girls.

For the past three years, Cole had wanted one thing—to get even with Caesar Kemble for cheating his daddy out of what was left of their ranch and for running his brother off. Those acres weren't just land to Cole. They'd been part of him. He'd dreamed of ranching them with his brother someday.

Not that his daddy gave much of a damn that the last of the land that had been a legendary ranch was gone.

"Leave it be, boy. It was my ranch, not yours. Maybe Caesar and me was both drunk as a pair of coons in a horse trough filled with whiskey, but Kemble won Black Oaks fair and square with that royal flush."

"The hell he did, Daddy. The hell he did. You were drunk because he got you drunk. Caesar Kemble knew exactly what he was doing. And another thing, Black Oaks wasn't just yours, either. You didn't have the right to gamble it away. It was mine and Shanghai's."

"Well, it's gone just the same, boy. You can't rewrite history. You're a loser, born to a loser, brother of a loser. History is always written by the winners."

"I swear—if it's the last thing I ever do, I'll get Black Oaks back."

"You'll get yourself killed if you mess with Caesar Kemble. That's what you'll do. My father was a hothead like you and he went over to have it out with the Kembles and vanished into thin air. Don't get yourself murdered, boy, or run off, like Shanghai did.''

"As if you care—''

His easygoing daddy hadn't cared much about anything other than partying and getting drunk.

With his Stetson low over his dark brow and longish black hair, Cole followed a well-worn dirt pathway through sandy pastures choked by huisache, ebony and mesquite. Dr. Pepper trotted for at least a mile before Cole's heart quickened when he saw the billowing dust from the herd rising above a stand of low trees like yellow smoke to dirty the sky.

The vaqueros and Kemble's sons, who worked for The Golden Spurs, had been gathering the herd for several days in the dense thickets that had once belonged to the Knights. Rich as he was, Caesar, who like Cole, loved cowboying more than he loved anything—including cheating at cards—would be out there with his men and sons. Cole hoped to catch him alone in some deep and thorny thicket and have it out with him.

Yes, sirree, that's just what he hoped until he saw Lizzy Kemble through the dense brush. Somehow the sight of the slim, uncertain girl on the tall, black gelding struggling to keep up with the vaqueros and her more able brothers, cousins and sister, stopped him cold.

Lizzy was fair-skinned, and didn't look like the rest of her family, who were a big-boned, tanned, muscular bunch—a bullying bunch who thought they were kings, who lorded it over everybody else in the four counties their ranch covered.

The spirited horse was too much for her, and she knew it. Her spine was stiff with fear. Anybody could see that. Her hands even shook. She was covered with dirt from head to toe, and her hat was as flat as a pancake on one side, which meant she'd already taken a tumble or two.

She might have seemed laughable to him if her eyes

weren't so big and her pretty, heart-shaped face so white. She looked scared to death and vulnerable, too. Sensing her fear, the gelding was stamping the ground edgily just itching for trouble.

Cole shook his head, ashamed for the girl and yet worried about her, too. What the hell was wrong with him? He should be glad Caesar Kemble's daughter was such a miserable failure as a cowgirl.

He had a mission. He should forget her, but Cole couldn't stop staring, his gaze fixing on her cute butt in those skintight jeans and then on the long, pale, mud-caked braid that swung down her back. Her breasts jiggled enticingly, too.

Not bad for jailbait.

His former glimpses of her in town hadn't done her justice. She'd grown up some since then, gotten herself a soft, curvaceous body and a woman's vulnerability that appealed to him much as he would have preferred to despise her. It didn't matter that she was a Kemble, nor that the Kembles had been swindling the Knights for more than a hundred years. Something about her big eyes made him feel powerful and want to protect her.

He forgot Caesar and concentrated on the girl, who didn't seem like she fit with her clan at all. All of a sudden his quest for revenge looked like it might take a much sweeter path than the one he'd originally intended.

But then that's how life is. You think you're fixed on where you're going—then you come to a tempting fork in the road that changes everything.

Lizzy Kemble looked mighty tempting….

Could she choose
between the navy
and love?

New York Times
bestselling author

DEBBIE MACOMBER

The return of her
famous NAVY series!

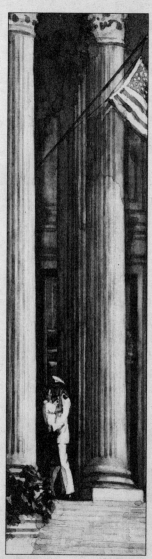

NAVY *Woman*

Despite the strictly
taboo laws of naval
fraternizing, navy attorney
Catherine Fredrickson
and her new boss,
Royce Nyland, find
themselves strongly
attracted. Just how long
will they be able to
resist each other...?

*Look for NAVY WOMAN
in July 2004.*

Silhouette®
Where love comes alive™

DYNASTIES: THE DANFORTHS

**A family of prominence...
tested by scandal, sustained by passion.**

COWBOY CRESCENDO

(Silhouette Desire #1591)

by Cathleen Galitz

Newly hired nanny Heather Burroughs quickly
won over Toby Danforth's young son with her
warmth and humor, but Toby's affection was
harder to tap into. This sizzling cowboy was
still reeling from his disastrous divorce and
certainly wasn't looking for a new bride.
Could Heather lasso this lone rancher
and get him to settle down?

*Available July 2004
at your favorite retail outlet.*

COMING NEXT MONTH

SDCNM0604